HALF-BLOOD ACADEMY 1:

MAGIC TRIALS

Meg Xuemei X

Copyright © 20109 by Meg Xuemei X

All rights reserved under the International and Pan-American Copyright Conventions. No part of this book may be reproduced or transmitted in any form or by any means, electronic or mechanical, including photocopying, recording, or by any information storage and retrieval system, without permission in writing from the publisher.

This is a work of fiction. Names, places, characters and incidents are either the product of the author's imagination or are used fictitiously, and any resemblance to any actual persons, living or dead, organizations, events or locales is entirely coincidental.

Warning: the unauthorized reproduction or distribution of this copyrighted work is illegal. Criminal copyright infringement, including infringement without monetary gain, is investigated by the FBI and is punishable by up to 5 years in prison and a fine of $250,000.

Cover art by Jay R Villalobos
Edited by Jax Garren
Proofread by Jane Beyer

First Edition
ISBN: 9781070880235

Printed in the United States of America

Half-Blood Academy 1: Magic Trials

The demigods can't decide if they want to screw me or kill me.

My name is Marigold. I'm a hunter living in the Great Merge—Lucifer has brought Hell to half of Earth, and four demigods rule the other half.

The smoking-hot Demigod of War rounded up my team to enroll them in Half-blood Academy, aka Half-death Academy, due to the survival rate of the students.

When he sees me, he wants no one else but me. So he offers to spare my team if I go in their place. Problem is, no human outside the bloodline of the gods can survive the magic trials. The demigod insists I'm anything but human, and he's willing to risk my life to find out what I'm made of.

I'm not the weakest link, even though all the bullies in the Academy mock me. I'm nothing anyone has ever seen before, and when my forbidden power awakens, the demigods will regret they ever tried to make me their bitch.

TABLE OF CONTENTS

Prologue 8
Chapter 1 18
Chapter 2 42
Chapter 3 53
Chapter 4 69
Chapter 5 81
Chapter 6 97
Chapter 7 118
Chapter 8 146
Chapter 9 156
Chapter 10 171
Chapter 11 193
Chapter 12 224
Chapter 13 231
Chapter 14 246
Chapter 15 249
Sneak Preview of A Court of Blood and Void 347
About the Author 368

Prologue
The Demigod of War

The green-eyed human girl fought like a fiend against a large, vicious gang.

Her ferocity was the most stunning thing I'd ever seen.

But I didn't come for her. We came for the two supernaturals on her team. Rogues weren't allowed to roam the demigods' territory unchecked. They either joined the Academy or were put down.

Wrap it up, I ordered Cameron, the lieutenant of the Dominion of Gods, with a gesture. These soldiers had survived the Trial of the Blood Runes because they had gods' blood in their veins.

The fight in the street ceased abruptly as Cameron's men marched into the battlefield, gunning for their targets. The other combatants stepped back, fear for the Dominion soldiers sinking in their eyes—all except for the human girl.

She stepped in front of a teenage wolf shifter and an underage witch, blocking Cameron and his soldiers.

"Marigold, they're the Dominions. We can't fight them off," the shifter whispered, trying to pull her back to protect her, but she shrugged him off.

"Like Hell I'll let them take you!" she said, her hands twitching, ready for violence.

She was still running on adrenaline. I smelled her dark fear, though it was no match for her fury.

Cameron's jaw clenched. He hadn't met a civilian who dared resist an arrest or recruitment. And no one cursed in front of a Dominion soldier without suffering the consequences.

The lieutenant and his men were more than zealous to impress me, as a demigod rarely accompanied them on an enlistment mission.

"I don't give a fuck how pretty you are, chick," Cameron snorted. "Get the fuck out of my way, or—"

The girl attacked.

She planted a boot into Cameron's chest and kicked hard. At the same time, she nocked five arrows, letting them fly in blurry succession.

Her every aim hit true, but she was up against the well-trained Dominion warriors in armor that no human weapon could penetrate.

Our forces surrounded her. The girl yelled for the shifter and witch to run, but instead they pressed their backs against hers, ready to fight to the death with her.

I chuckled.

"Fun's over, little minx," I said, peeling myself from the shade and stepping into the battlefield before my soldiers terminated the trio.

My demigod power coiled, ripping the fabric of the air.

Every knee—the soldiers', the civilians', and the gang members'—dropped to a battlefield strewn with shells of bullets, bits of concrete, animal fur, and blood.

Yet one pair of knees refused to go down.

A flick of surprise flashed through my eyes. That was a first.

The girl braced her feet apart and glared at me, the fire of fury burning in her eyes, their color so vivid it was greener than any forest in any universe I'd passed.

A flame lashed out like invisible lightning, striking the icy, steel walls that encased my careless, ruthless demigod heart.

Instantly, my cock hardened.

What the fuck?

The beast roared in me, awakening, as did my primal need.

I reined in the beast with effort so I wouldn't drag down that female, push her to the ground, and mount her from behind, right there.

I prided myself in not being a savage demigod, but without a mirror, I knew my eyes glowed molten gold with a crimson ring around the pupils.

My power increased, unleashing at the girl's challenge. Violent wind charged from me, wheeling and slamming into everything in its path.

The buildings within the scope of my power rumbled, glass shattering.

The wolves, hybrids, and humans whimpered as they were thrown backwards, including the young witch and the shifter who knelt behind the human girl.

She swayed before steadying herself.

Kneel, I commanded her.

Her lavender hair spread wildly, whipped by the electrifying power in the air. Beads of sweat dotted on her cute little nose. Fear and rage spoke volumes in her eyes as she endeavored to resist my power.

Her legs buckled, revealing her human weakness, and I waited for her to drop to her knees to pay me respect, like everyone else.

My faint smile wilted from the corners of my lips when she straightened her back and straightened her legs.

No human or supernatural could withstand my compulsion, except for the primordial Olympian gods and Lucifer. Even my demigod peers had to put on their armor and shield themselves against me with their power.

But this mere human girl stood her ground.

As if that wasn't infuriating enough, she flipped me the bird.

It was the first time anyone had ever given me that. She didn't know she was courting violence, then death.

My soldiers' gasps were audible, even over the gang's and her companions'. Hushed quietness resumed at my snarl.

Everyone waited for me to strike down the insolent human girl.

The minx smirked, the brightest, most gorgeous thing on Earth, and every predatory cell within me swirled alive.

A thrill coursed through my veins.

My cock grew hard, jerking forward and rasping painfully against the fabric of my pants.

I clenched my teeth, willing myself to keep control and stay put, no matter how badly I wanted to claim this female now, over and over.

Fortunately, instead of tight armor, I wore a leather trench coat, which covered my erection.

My gaze roved over her sinfully enticing body before peering into her eyes to search for her secrets—how could a human oppose me?

What was she?

I stalked toward the deadly, beautiful creature, hands in my pockets as if I were strolling in the park. Despite my casual manner, another wave of whimpers from the soldiers and gang members indicated the effects of my rippling power.

The girl tensed at my approach, the knuckles of one hand white on her spear and her other hand ready to, I assume, pull out a gun from her leather jacket to turn on me.

I held her blazing gaze, daring her to try.

Her fear blended with hate and fascination, wheeling in her fiery jade eyes as she kept glaring at me.

The minx wasn't entirely immune to me and my power, after all.

I held back an amused chortle. It was rare anyone could still amuse me, even though I was the youngest demigod walking Earth.

And I had never been so aroused.

She didn't back off but held her chin high and puffed up her chest, which drew my gaze to her perky breasts.

I strode around her, studying her as if she were a prickly kitten I'd cornered, and she wheeled accordingly, never showing her back to me.

When I'd annoyed her enough, she gave in, breaking the silence.

"What the fuck do you want, demigod?" she demanded. "And which demigod are you?"

Such attitude. Outlaws always hated authorities.

Everyone else held their breath at her lack of self-preservation. I would have squashed the offender had it been anyone less interesting.

I didn't bother to conceal a flick of surprise.

Everyone else knew who I was. She must be terribly isolated in this forsaken town. Yet she knew I was a half-blood.

I tilted my head and sniffed. A discovery made my eyes brighten, and I smiled. She wasn't the human she presented herself to be.

Yet she wasn't like anything I'd encountered.

This close, I could sense potent power in her bloodstream, but it was veiled.

She didn't even know, or she'd have fought with her magic instead of rudimentary bows and daggers.

Some force held her magic captive.

Then her scent hit me fully in the face, and waves of heat rushed inside me until they all gathered in my groin.

A firestorm of lust burned in my veins.

That instant I decided what she would be for me.

She was the puzzle I needed to solve.

A wilderness to tame.

A treasure I'd found.

A rare jewel I would possess and lock in the most guarded vault.

And a female I would ride every night, savoring her cries as she begged for the ecstasy I could give her. This girl I would claim as my mate.

The mystic wind passed between us, and she widened her stunningly green eyes as if she'd seen the most brilliant sunlight flooding the forest for the first time. She'd taken in my scent as well, and I watched her reaction in satisfaction.

Her soft, full lips parted with shock. She'd fight me with every ounce of her strength if I told her now that she was mine and her future belonged with me.

She recovered faster than I'd thought any woman could.

But then, she wasn't just any woman. Not even close.

"We're law-abiding citizens, mister. You won't take any member of my coven," she shouted, then swept her spearhead toward the werewolf gang she'd fought. "But you're more than welcome to round up those up-to-no-good scumbags! They should fight the demons in the frontier at your Dominions' command instead of harassing innocent small-town people."

The werewolves snarled, but stopped the instant Cameron shot them a harsh look.

"They're too old," Cameron said, thrusting his chin toward the werewolves before training his hard gaze on the girl. "Only the teenage wolf and witch will be enrolled into the Academy. We came for them, so I suggest you step aside if you don't want any more trouble."

He was nicer to the girl, though wary, after she'd put up a fight against me.

"No way!" the girl said. "Everyone knows Half-Blood Academy is actually Half-Death Academy. Less than half of the attendants survive the first ritual, and I won't let my people try their luck."

"How dare you!" Cameron hissed. "That blasphemy alone shall get you hanged."

I raised a hand to stop Cameron from cursing the girl further and quirked an eyebrow at her. It'd be interesting to see how the fiery minx survived her first day at my academy.

"I'll spare your friends under one condition," I said with a charming smile that every woman ate up.

She narrowed her eyes, but I could feel her pulse spike.

Her every reaction provoked mine, exciting me.

The girl arched a long, elegant eyebrow, relaxing a little and ready to bargain.

"And what is your condition, demigod?"

"You go in their places, Marigold," I said.

CHAPTER 1
Marigold

I burst through the twisted trees in the dim forest, stealth no longer necessary or possible.

Jasper, the nineteen-year-old shifter in his white wolf form, had flushed out our prey and driven a pair of shimeras toward me.

Though we all preferred a rabbit's tender meat to roasted shimera, we were thinking long-term. The shimera grew in number, faster than any other mutant beasts. We couldn't afford to let them move out of the forest and overrun the blocks where Jasper, Circe—a seventeen-year-old witch—and I had taken up residence for the last three years.

The old, warded library building had been our last frontier, ever since the age of the Great Merge, when the world fell and was divided between the demons and four demigods.

Their unceasing war afflicted nearly every earthling and every corner of Earth.

We were lucky to have this town, called Crack, which the hordes of demons and the Dominion army of the demigods neglected or had forgotten while they were busy fighting for richer land.

That was why Jasper, Circe, and I had stayed here, and we stuck together to survive.

The shimera pair swiveled in my direction, their fur gray and fangs sharp. The species had a bull's shape and a kitten's size. But only idiots were fooled by their small form. They were some of the most vicious beasts in the jungle.

The pair leapt my way, mouths open to toast me. The little beasts' fire was deadly within seven feet, hence Jasper had kept his distance while driving them in my direction.

"Watch out!" Circe warned from my left flank, moving to cover my back, her boots stomping on the dried leaves and twigs behind me.

I winced at her novice mistake, but then I had to cut her some slack. She'd just started hunting with Jasper and me. My young witch friend had begged me over and over, claiming that she was old enough to join our hunt and promising to be useful.

"I'm only two and half years younger than you and one and half younger than Jasper," she had said crossly. "You aren't my mother! If you want to protect me, you'll need to prepare me for this fucked-up world. And don't treat me as the weakest link amid the three of us."

But she *was* the weakest among the three of us.

She'd seemed to read my thought and raised her chin. "I might not be as fast and strong as you, Marigold, but it won't always be that way." She'd even put a hand on her hip to emphasize her point. "You're only a human, but I'm a witch. I have way more magic than you can ever have. I'll be more powerful when I reach your age."

Jasper had shot her a glare. He was a peaceful wolf shifter and didn't like any discord among us. "Be grateful that Marigold took us in," he'd warned.

"I'm not being disrespectful." Circe glared back at him. The two always argued when they didn't have anyone else to fight with. Circe was in a teenage rebellion stage, despite that she loved me. I hadn't had the luxury, though, to go through that same phase. She kept going. "I was merely stating a fact. Marigold can deal with truth. If anything, she always appreciates honesty."

I'd finally caved in. No matter how much I wanted to shield her, we lived in a dangerous world, and she needed to have all sorts of survival skill sets.

I was older and led the pack, but as they were supernaturals, soon their powers would surpass mine. Our hierarchy was going to change irrevocably when that happened.

Would I be a follower and let one of them lead?

Being a follower wasn't in my blood.

I shook off the thought of what our future would become and focused on the game.

I assigned Circe to be my shadow. Her role was to confuse bigger predators by sending our scent in the opposite direction with her homebrew spells.

A rapid stream of fire poured out from between the shimeras' serrated fangs.

I'd underestimated the beasts' speed. Though we'd hunted them for a while, the shimera, being mutants, had upgraded.

Jasper, the wolf, rushed toward us from behind the beasts, yelping in warning.

I was in the direct path of the beasts' fire.

If I'd hunted alone, it'd be easy to sidestep the shimeras' fire stream, but Circe was right behind me. If I lunged or ducked, the fire would hit her.

I threw myself backward, slamming the young witch to the ground with me. At the same time, I sent my arrows flying, three of them at once. Each hit a shimera's eye.

The buggers had also underestimated me. They'd thought their twin fires would barbeque a dinner. But the pair had been quite good. It'd been a close call. I'd felt the heat of their fire.

Circe whimpered while my body still shielded her.

I was up in an instant and gave her a hand. She scrambled up when Jasper reached us.

We didn't take time to savor our victory or regard the fallen shimeras with my arrows pierced through their skulls.

Circe and I quickly stuffed our hunt into a backpack while Jasper stood guard. We were ready to leave the forest before the witch's spells lost effect and the bigger predators followed our trail.

I grinned at Jasper and Circe. We would have full stomachs tonight, and we could trade the other shimera for a loaf of bread and a bag of potatoes.

Despite the fact that the three of us could hunt, we kept it to once a week. We were the only hunter team in Crack that still came out of the woods, and none of us wanted to take more risks than necessary.

The thought of dinner made my stomach grumble. Circe smirked at me, elbowing my belly teasingly, and Jasper rolled out his pink tongue, his way of laughing.

Suddenly my back stiffened.

Foreboding sent a chill up my spine. Then a heat wave, like invisible fire, chased away the chill that had so quickly sunk into my bones.

The sensation was so unfamiliar and terrifying that for a moment, I almost thought I had magic.

The stench of brimstone, sulfur, and acid hit my nostrils. Jasper stared at me with a question. Then next, he tensed, his light amber eyes turning dark.

Something was hunting us.

I straightened slowly, my eyes searching the dark. Even though I was a human, I seemed to have better night vision than average.

I met a pair of red eyes between the brown trees.

Darkness whirled in the demon's eyes, hungry to devour every light and possess every bit of soul until the monster had drained his victim completely.

I swallowed with difficulty.

I'd survived the streets on my own until I was ten, when Vi took me in and trained me to be a hunter. She'd drilled the necessity of staying the hell away from both demons and gods and never ever letting either one get close.

I'd never questioned her edict. What Vi had warned me was common sense—even a fool would avoid this planet's two top predators.

Thinking of Vi brought a sharp pain and longing to my chest. She'd given me, a stranded street rat, a home. But after four years, she'd disappeared without a word, leaving no trace. I'd searched the entire Crack for her and almost hadn't made it out when I'd then scoured the forest.

Gradually I'd accepted that I'd been dumped again, just as my parents had abandoned me to the streets before I was old enough to remember them.

I'd inherited Vi's old library since then, and her ward had prevented anyone or any creature from getting into it except the ones invited by me. After living and hunting alone for two years, I'd rescued Jasper and Circe from a brutal criminal lord, who no longer breathed, and they'd become my people ever since.

I dragged my memory away from my old guardian and the aching sense of loss she'd left behind. Across the dark space, I stared at the demon.

He had long, dark horns, black eyes, and red lips.

This was a grade three demon in their power hierarchy. The highest rank was ten, and that would be Lucifer. I blinked, not sure why suddenly I had this knowledge, since it was the first time I'd seen a demon so close.

His obsidian gaze met mine, and shock flitted by his eyes.

He sniffed the air, and a dark mass swirled out of the pits of his eyes, hunger and craving sparking like hellfire in them.

He fixated only on me, not bothering to even glance at Circe or Jasper.

They'd both spotted the demon and frozen in fear.

"Retreat slowly," I whispered and led by example as I backed toward a tree.

Circe blinked, as if waking up from a trance at my order.

"Conceal. Uttar Sloan Samish Rota conceal," Circe murmured her chant frantically, trying to get us to melt into the trees and thus avoid the demon's detection.

The demon grinned at me and uttered a demonic word, which blurred into the black wind. It sounded familiar, but any chance at comprehension was drowned out by the pounding rhythm of my frenetic heartbeat in my ears.

Circe's concealing spell evidently had no effect on the creature since he kept stalking toward me, sniffing the air as if it was filled with nectar.

Stop! Demon, stop! I hissed silently.

The demon halted for a second, as if confused or uncertain.

Circe repeated her chanting and tossed out a few spells, which appeared around us in the shapes of balls and stars.

The demon shrugged them off and flicked his claws to show us what he had.

A demonic power, also familiar, like something once featured in my nightmares, exuded from him. Its dark force drew us toward him, like a spider that intends to numb its victims before consuming them.

If a third degree demon could do this, what chance did we have to fight a full-blown demon? Horror flickered through my mind. Vi hadn't been wrong to warn me to stay clear of Lucifer's pawns.

Circe and Jasper now both glided toward the demon as if in a dream. The Hell-creature widened his grin.

"What on Earth are you two doing?" I yelled at them. Our cover was blown anyway. I pinched Circe on the arm and swatted Jasper's snout. "Run! Like your asses are on fire."

If the demon possessed any one of us, all three of us would be done for.

I dragged Circe and kicked Jasper. Relief wound through me as they returned to their senses, and three of us darted away between the trees in a mad dash.

The demon gave chase, giggling.

He zoomed in on us.

Jasper raced beside me, keeping up, but then we both realized that Circe had lagged behind. Terror hit me, and I turned just in time to see the demon rake his claws toward Circe's neck.

"You won't hurt her!" I screamed in rage and flung up my hands toward the demon, even though I was ten yards away and had no magic.

It was an instinct, a reflex. I reacted in panic.

I'd lost Vi. I couldn't lose either Circe or Jasper. They were all I had.

A blast of dark flame materialized above the demon, descending upon him before he could flee. The fire engulfed the creature.

It shrieked, and I clenched my teeth as his screams beat into my eardrums.

"Shut the fuck up and die!" I yelled.

The blaze plunged to the ground, sinking under and dragging the demon with it. Or maybe the flame actually burned the demon to ashes.

I didn't see a pile of cinders on the forest floor, though there was a circle burned into the ground, indicating where the magical conflagration had taken down a demon.

I sprang toward the young witch.

"Are you all right, Circe?" I asked, sounding like a mother even to my own ears.

She threw herself into my arms, trembling.

I stroked her back gently.

"Shush, you're safe now," I said. "We're all safe. Now let's get out of here."

I pulled Circe to sprint with me since her legs wobbled. Seeing the demon had shocked her. I didn't blame her. The appearance of the demon had shattered me as well.

Jasper kept pace, guarding and protecting us. His piercing wolf eyes darted around, his ears pricking backward as he scanned for any new danger.

I didn't allow us to slow down, even though the scent of smoke lingered on my tongue and the air burned in my lungs.

As soon as we shot out of the last line of trees, crossing the boundary into the town's territory, Jasper shifted. I knew he wanted to talk and demand answers regarding the flame that incinerated the demon, but I was just as baffled as he was.

One second he was still a wolf, then the next he was a good-looking teenage boy.

I glanced at him enviously. Being a shifter must be amazing.

The monsters usually didn't cross the boundary of the forest into the town's land during daytime. I'd wondered if Vi ever set a ward along the boundary.

Circe tossed Jasper a stack of clothes from the outside pocket of her backpack, and he snatched them from the air. In no time, he had his trousers on and his muscled chest pressed against an old T-shirt.

The witch's gaze lingered on his cut chest a bit too long before she tore it away. The shifter was eye candy with dark, curly hair and rich brown eyes, and he always had a good laugh.

She'd developed a crush on him after her seventeenth birthday two months ago. It was fine with me if they hooked up. I couldn't think of a better man to protect her.

I sighed. They'd grown up, and I was getting older.

Jasper didn't notice Circe's heated gaze before she disguised it. His concerned, sharp expression fixed on my face, uncompromising.

I waved a hand to signal for him to let me have a break and set my palms on my knees to brace myself. I bent from my waist, panting laboriously at the ground. Circe did the same. I took a little comfort that, even though she was younger, she was breathing louder.

When I finally straightened, I grinned at them. We'd survived once again, together.

"Guys, do you want to high five or a group hug?" I asked.

My motto was that every victory, no matter how small, should be celebrated so we would prowl on through life and never get beaten down.

Circe rolled her eyes. In her delusional mind, she thought she was more mature than I. But I understood that she wanted to keep that image in front of Jasper. At some point, I might need to talk to her, as she considered me competition more often than not.

Perhaps that was the problem with only one male in a pack.

Jasper obliged me and hit my palm with his rough one for a high five before we jogged down a long street toward the old, abandoned library—our residence—several blocks away.

The metal dish glinted in autumn's sunlight at the top of the brown building, beckoning us to return home. That was always a comforting sight.

"We've never had a demon in this forest before." Jasper started, strolling to my left.

"We almost became the demon's snack today," Circe said, large eyes peeking at Jasper. "Did you hear its laughter? It chilled me to the bone. If any more of them come, Crack won't be safe for us anymore. Where can we go next?"

Worry knotted in my stomach.

We'd never lingered in the forest long enough for any monsters to ambush us. Each of us played a different role—Jasper flushed out game, I shot them, and Circe used her spells to cover our scent so we could leave the scene quickly once we'd grabbed the game.

We'd never had a demon complication before.

We weren't equipped to deal with a demon. We might not be lucky again if another Hell-creature, especially a more powerful one, showed up in town.

However, the flame had appeared out of nowhere and burned the demon. The demonic being had vanished without a trace after it screamed, as if it had been dragged back to Hell.

But the realm of Hell had already merged with half of Earth's surface, which was Lucifer's greatest achievement. Somehow he'd broken the seal and the boundary after eons of confinement in the endless inferno. And now he sought to bring the full Hell to Earth. Only the God of War and his four demigods held on, refusing to give up their reign on the other half of the planet.

"You have magic, Marigold," Jasper drawled. "It was powerful enough to banish a demon. And all this time you thought you were just a human."

"But I am a human," I said, staring down at my hands and willing a spark of fire to manifest, to give some evidence that the flame had indeed blasted out of me and prove that I might be something more.

I'd felt energy surge through me when the flame appeared, but it could've been my imagination. I'd tasted fire and smoke on the back of my tongue, but it could've just been the burning air.

Right now, not even an ember answered my call.

I shook my head. "I couldn't have the kind of fire that could burn a grade-three demon."

"How did you know that demon's power grade?" Jasper asked.

"Uh…" I blinked. "I thought everyone could tell."

"We couldn't," Jasper said. "I think your need to protect us and your intense reaction to the demon threat brought out your power."

"Or the flame could have come from Circe," I said, turning to my witch friend. "Did you feel like it generated from you? You've been practicing fire spells."

She bit her plump lower lip and mused for a second before she nodded. "It could've. I've cast fire spells before, though nothing as big as that. But when facing the demon, I could have enhanced the flame. I felt the power blast in the air. Everything happened so fast I couldn't trace my spells. I need to practice more on my power to conjure up fire at will."

I nodded in approval. "You're a natural, Circe. We can clean up the courtyard for you to practice."

Circe beamed.

Jasper gave me an unreadable glance, but he didn't look convinced that the flame was Circe's witch fire.

"What do you guys need?" I asked, changing subject. "You two go ahead and stew the shimera." Jasper was the best cook among us, so cooking was his lot. I grabbed my backpack. "I'll go take the other shimera to the market."

"Maybe I should go to the trade?" Jasper said, concern in his brown eyes.

"No way," I said. "I'm the best trader, and you don't even bargain much." I knew he was worried that I might get attacked alone. I grinned at him. "I know all the shortcuts, and I run damn fast. No one enjoys messing with me."

Jasper gave me an appreciative look. "You're a vicious fighter, and everyone who isn't awfully dumb has learned that you're also vengeful."

"Hey, be careful with my reputation," I said.

"You can take me with you, you know," Circe said. "I can watch your back."

She wanted to escape the chore of skinning the shimera.

I smirked. "Go home, kids."

I waved goodbye.

The next second I tensed, sensing a new threat.

Jasper growled as if he'd felt it, too—the looming of predators.

Circe widened her nervous eyes. "What now?" She grabbed the three remaining spells from her pocket. "We can't deal with another demon attack."

"Run!" I yelled.

All three of us burst toward the warded library.

Only a few more blocks and three more turns and we'd reach the building. We had more weapons in our dwelling.

Movements blurred all around us.

A pack of six werewolves intercepted us from two opposite corners, four of them in werewolf form. As one, the three of us swerved in another direction, only to meet a gang of a dozen armed humans blocking the other end of the alley.

Crack wasn't a bad place to live, as it wasn't in the grasp of either the demons or the demigods. The only downside was that horrible humans and rogue supernaturals kept migrating to this settlement, and some decided to rule this patch of land.

They usually fought in the town's center. Few of them ventured into the edges where monsters took the dark forest and the three of us occupied an abandoned library.

The old gangs basically left me alone, my crazy reputation encouraging them to give me a wide berth.

But this time, instead of avoiding me, they'd decided to gang up on me.

The three of us halted in the middle of an ambush and pressed our backs against each other.

Snarling, Jasper tore his T-shirt off and shifted in an instant.

Circe hissed, her shaking hands tight on the three spells she had left.

I flashed my usual syrupy smile, regarding the werewolf pack that appeared to be a bigger threat before flicking my reckless glance toward the human gang who still feared and resented me.

"Hello, David, right?" I purred, making eye contact with a rough-looking human leader in his thirties. His left ear was missing, and I might have had something to do with that. From how he glared at me, I'd bet he hadn't forgotten the incident and he wasn't going to forgive me any time soon.

"I see you don't wear a hat anymore," I continued. "And you've made new friends. How courteous of you to introduce us to your big ass supernatural friends."

The scar on David's left cheek twitched, and I might have contributed to that long scar, too. Well, he wasn't friendly to many women. I'd gotten caught up in the moment and defended them after I decided that he couldn't be persuaded to be a bit more polite.

"Shut up, you crazy bitch!" David spat, but he had bad aim, and his second-in-command—what was his name, Jason?—was a bit too slow to avoid getting hit.

Jason winced and subtly withdrew a half-step, not interested in a second serving from his unstable boss.

"Today is your doom, bitch!" David declared.

"Haven't heard the B word for a while," I said, stalling so Jasper could have more time to recover and gather strength from his shifting and Circe could find a better chanting spell. She didn't do well under stress, so I had to keep this as anxiety-free as possible. And I was still eyeing all the possible exits. "I kind of missed the name calling. By the way, have you heeded my advice and given the name David to someone else? David is a nice, meek male name that only suits—"

"Enough!" the werewolf alpha barked. Just like any alpha male, he wasn't keen on letting someone else take the limelight.

I slid him a sidelong glance.

In his human form, he was bulky and shorter than I expected for a pack alpha. He also had greasy hair, which I didn't like. Man, if you wanted to lead, at least set an example for your minions on hygiene.

But voicing that opinion would get me attacked right away.

He pointed his thick index finger at me, and the tip was a bit yellowish. "Is this the nasty bitch you told me about, David?"

I sighed audibly. So far, I'd smiled at all of them, and my smile was sweet. I knew that since I'd practiced it before the mirror. So it wasn't me. It was them.

I hated to say this, but the alpha didn't impress me. But I couldn't remember any male who ever left a good impression on me, except for Jasper.

"Yes, Alpha Rocco," David said, and he even bowed a little.

I wasn't a fan of that name either, but he might not want my advice on changing his name.

"That's the mad-cow bitch," David added. This was the fourth time someone had called me a bitch today. Just my luck. "I promise you she'll fetch a top price at market after your men have their way with her."

My heart skipped a beat. While I was busy hunting and living my own life, the criminal lords in Crack had gotten into the human trafficking business?

I met Rocco's nefarious, dominant stare. He growled when I didn't avert my gaze, which reminded me of the customs of the shifter packs. They had this submissive game that required anyone who was lesser than an alpha to lower their gaze, unless they wanted to challenge the alpha.

I was sick and tired of all this bullshit, especially when they should have just let Jasper and Circe go home to make stew and let me go to the market to trade for some necessities instead of harassing us.

I was in a bad mood now. So, no, I had no intention of looking away or lowering my eyes.

I had as much right as he to look anyone in the eyes and keep looking.

Werewolf magic rolled off the alpha, demanding attention. The human gang members dropped their gazes to the ground. The pack members in their human forms dropped to one knee in submission, and the ones in werewolf form lowered themselves and bowed their heads.

This wasn't a weak alpha, which made me think of all the lives he'd had to snuff out to rise to the top of the pack.

Even Jasper wanted to lower his head, and Circe shook behind me, both under the influence of his power.

That enraged me.

I brushed off his werewolf vibe and stared at him harder, but added a sardonic smile. A flick of surprise flitted through his eyes, soon replaced by anger and the promise of punishment.

"Surrender now, bitches," the werewolf alpha demanded, "and I'll let you live to serve me and my pack as our whores. Resist, and we'll tear you limb from limb."

Jasper snarled. I bumped his head with my hip to tell him to hold back.

David snickered in vile delight. He thought he'd brought the bigger gun and finally had a chance to get back at me. He'd called this day my doom day.

"Hey, Rocco, right?" I asked. "How are you doing? Do you smoke?"

"What?" he snarled, trying not to appear confused by my question or my boldness. "Are you stupid or what?"

"I'm not stupid, but I'm curious," I said. "If you aren't a smoker, how come your fingers are so yellow? Also, as a woman, I don't appreciate being called a whore. I'm not too pleased to have been called a bitch four times today either. In a nutshell, I don't like the way you treat women."

Like a flash, I drew a gun from the inside of my leather coat and shot the alpha between the eyes.

It was either that or be dragged off and sold as a whore.

I didn't wait to see if he dropped in a heap or not and wheeled toward the human gangs.

I fired five shots in rapid succession. While talking to David, I'd made a mental note on who carried guns. So, the gunmen had to go first.

David didn't get a chance to call me a crazy bitch one last time before he closed his eyes and died.

"Didn't expect this, dicks?" I murmured. "I'm full of surprises."

I'd tried not to waste bullets, since they were costly, but we were outnumbered and I wouldn't take a chance of getting Jasper and Circe killed.

Extreme circumstance required extreme actions.

I slipped my gun into a holster around my hips, pulled two daggers, and hurled them at two werewolves. I didn't stop there as two more of my daggers followed suit.

I'd packed a dozen daggers for hunting—that was my style. I wasn't exactly a trigger-happy kind of chick, but I could never be faulted for being prepared.

Jasper crashed into a massive werewolf who'd been wounded by my dagger. They locked jaws, snarling, pounding, biting, and clawing with animal brutality.

Circe threw her spells at the remaining humans and werewolves without discrimination. Purple smoke rose from one, and I prayed that she'd tossed the right spell this time.

Yells, curses, tearing sounds, and steel crossing steel echoed all around.

"Sorry, dudes," I shouted at my foes amid the chaos. "I forgot to warn you first. I know I'm a crazy bitch, but you should not mess with this crazy."

I smashed into a werewolf with a spear, a diabolic grin on my face.

A formidable force shook the street, instantly wiping away the smile twisting my lips.

I sliced at my opponent again and leapt as far away from the werewolf as I could, ignoring his furious bellow.

A bigger predator, the worst I'd ever felt, had arrived among us.

CHAPTER 2

The fighting ceased as seven Dominion soldiers stepped onto the battlefield as if they owned it.

A dark foreboding seized me.

Right as I'd thought we could get out of this battle intact, a more powerful predator had appeared, and I had a hunch why.

Shit would go down.

I licked my lips and pulled my beloved bow from my shoulder.

"Stand down!" their ringleader shouted at us, his voice stern and manner imperious. "Don't make any stupid moves if you want to remain in one piece."

I rolled my eyes at his idiotic turn of phrase. Why wouldn't anyone want to remain in one piece?

The Dominion soldiers surrounded us.

They hadn't trained any weapons on us yet, showing they didn't consider us a threat. I bet they could shoot faster than we could react. After all, they were elite Dominions, all of whom had the immortal gods' blood in their veins.

Based on the three-bar badge on the leading man's arm and an insignia of an eagle piercing through lightning on the chest of his armored uniform, I'd say he was a lieutenant.

Hazel eyes surveyed the remains of our fight from a hard face. Like all his soldiers, his hair had been cropped military short. The lieutenant flaunted his authority, but the formidable power I'd sensed earlier didn't come from him.

My eyes searched for the source, but the lieutenant wasn't kind enough to give me time to scan the newcomers. He stalked directly toward Jasper and Circe.

My chest tightened as my blood ran cold. The Dominions had come to take them away.

I stepped forward and blocked him. "You're not taking them."

Everyone gasped at my audacity, but I didn't give a fuck.

I wouldn't lose Jasper and Circe, but I also knew we might not get out of this crisis this time.

The ringleader's face only hardened. "I don't give a fuck how pretty you are, chick," he snorted. "Get the fuck out of my way, or—"

At least he didn't call me bitch, which was a nice change.

But I was done being nice. I was done being pushed around and being afraid all the time that one day either the demons or the demigods' army would come to take the last of my family away from me.

I kicked the lieutenant in the chest. While he staggered back, surprised and angered, I let five arrows fly toward him and his soldiers.

"Run!" I shouted at Jasper and Circe.

But the stupid kids only formed up behind me, refusing to leave, despite me growling at them for their disobedience.

My arrows had no effect on the gods' soldiers.

The Dominion lieutenant lunged toward me with a sword, only to halt midway.

He stepped back.

"Fun's over, little minx," a rich male voice said, and a shiver of pleasure ran down my spine, making me want to purr.

What the fuck?

A giant, masculine male built like a gorgeous statue of bronze strode toward me like he had just descended from the glorious Heavens.

I glanced at his feet to check if he rode on a chariot of fire before returning my gaze to his face. His light amber eyes laughed at me as mine traced the curve of his mouth.

For a fleeting second, all I wanted was to lunge at him to lick his lips. I also wanted to trace my fingers along his cut chest inside his long, black leather coat.

I blinked back to my senses and frowned at him.

He was the sole owner of the predatory power I'd detected earlier.

A human should not be able to sense any magic, yet I had this cunning ability—be it a blessing or curse—to not just sense it, but tell its type and grade. For some reason, though, I couldn't categorize this man's power. I blamed it on my lack of experience. I hadn't seen much of the world.

I could tell, however, that this dangerous specimen contained top-of-the-line, ninth-degree power, which had to make him a demigod. Ten was reserved for Lucifer and the pureblood gods.

His power sang in my blood, as if calling to my own power, but I had no magic.

Vi had warned me to stay far away from any demon or demigod. It was too late now since I was facing a very powerful one right in front of me.

But I did not fear this demigod—who seemed to terrify everyone else because all round me knees went down and hit the dirty ground.

"Did you just call me minx?" I demanded, trying to make him feel bad for being a jerk. There might be a chance I could talk my way out of here. This demigod had stopped his lieutenant from attacking me with a scary sword. "No one calls me minx. I hunt and eat minx."

He chuckled, as if my defiance only amused him, and that sexy male sound made my toes curl. Good thing he couldn't see my body's reaction. Add one more thing boots were good for—hiding how suddenly and completely turned on I was.

His gaze dropped to my lips for a heartbeat before returning to peek into my eyes, potent magic in his probe.

I stared back at him, holding my ground.

His face, playful a moment ago, turned steel hard.

As power rolled off him, a brutal wind whipped around me, screwing up my facial expression and tossing my lavender hair about.

Now I would have to comb my hair again!

The wind didn't make me shake in my boots, but it rumbled the old library blocks away. If the remaining glass shattered because he'd thrown a fit, he'd have to cover expenses for the repair. I'd send the bill to the Half-Blood Academy, where the demigods resided, according to rumor.

His magical wind threw everyone else backward, but it didn't work on me.

Had he spared me alone, or was I simply so awesome that I could resist his power?

I got the answer when he silently commanded me, *Kneel.*

The word of power slammed into my mind, and I desired nothing more than to drop to my knees and show him my soft belly in submission.

But I wasn't that kind of girl. His manhandling only infuriated me.

I braced my feet apart and glared at him. His eyes turned molten gold at the defiant fire in my eyes.

I'd truly pissed off a demigod.

A small yelping sound from Circe and Jasper confirmed just that. I'd help them up after I dealt with this asshole.

All gods, demigods, and demons were merciless psychopaths. There was no difference between them. Just look at how they tore the world apart with their male egos and wars.

There was no good guy on either side.

I braced for a blow from the demigod. I wasn't his match, and my daggers and arrows wouldn't do a damn thing to him, but I would still put up a fight.

His power increased, and I felt like the weight of a truck landed on my slender shoulders.

Cold sweat dampened my armpits.

A cocky smile tugged the demigod's lips as he waited for me to drop to my knees in front of him, but I was one hell of a stubborn chick.

I refused to bow or kneel to anyone.

Be gone. You'll not crush me! I screamed at the weight, and then suddenly it was lifted. I felt light as a feather.

What's happening?

Even since I'd met and possibly vanquished that demon, I seemed to possess some magic. My words commanded power. Maybe I'd stolen the demon's power without knowing it?

That was cool if there were no side effects.

So giddy that I'd resisted a demigod's compulsion, I flipped him the bird.

Everyone who saw my finger gasped.

Had no one ever shown a demigod a vulgar gesture? I might be bold and aggressive, but I wasn't crazy enough to be suicidal. I just often acted and reacted before I thought things through.

It was too late to undo the damage now, but I dropped my hands and placed them on my hips.

A dark, voracious light flashed through his bright golden eyes.

So I smiled at him, sending him a signal that I could be nice, too, if he wanted to be friendly.

It must've worked because he didn't strike me but met my gaze as if I were the only person in the world. Then his eyes roamed my every inch.

That cherishing gaze made me so hot I nearly purred like a kitten being scratched under her chin. A current of electricity sparked between us, and pleasure buzzed over my skin.

Was that what people called chemistry?

The demigod stalked closer, his hands stuck in his pockets to show how harmless he was. That gesture wouldn't fool me. He could attack with a thought. I knew how dangerous he still was.

I prickled at his proximity, and dread seeped through my body.

Automatically, my knuckles went white on the hilt of my spear, and my other hand moved toward my gun, the cold metal a comfort against my warm fingers.

A challenge rose in his vicious, yet sexy eyes. Contrary to how I'd handled the other hooligans, I wouldn't be foolish enough to attack a demigod first. You couldn't kill a godly creature with a bullet or even dark magic.

And I didn't want to kill him. I wanted to do something else to him.

I reined in my wanton thoughts.

A hot ember sparked like dragon fire in the demigod's eyes. He enjoyed making me nervous, savoring my carnal reactions to his presence. But I didn't intend to show him anymore weakness, including this sudden, absurd lust.

I held my chin high.

He strolled around me, intentionally, just to get another reaction out of me or simply to annoy me. I wheeled accordingly, staring him in the eyes, never showing him my back.

"Which demigod are you?" I demanded.

I knew currently there were four demigods ruling half of the Earth, but I didn't know who this one was.

Instead of answering, he cocked his head to the side and sniffed me.

"Hey!" I shouted. I considered that an insult. I wasn't to be sniffed. I'd hunted in the forest today. I'd run from the demon. I'd fought werewolves and gangs. So naturally, I smelled sweaty. I'd intended to take a shower after the market visit, but my plans had been interrupted by all these uninvited interactions.

His gaze brightened like the stars, and in the reflection of his golden eyes, I saw mine also light up. But I didn't like the way he drew me to his flame. I didn't like losing control, and this demigod was making me nuts.

"We're law-abiding citizens, mister," I said, sweeping my spear until its head pointed right at the werewolves. "You won't take any member of my coven, but you're more than welcome to round up those up-to-no-good scumbags. They should fight the demons in the frontier at your Dominions' command instead of harassing innocent small-town people."

The surviving werewolves snarled their disagreement, but stopped at the Dominion soldiers' hisses. They were the biggest asses now.

"They're too old," the Dominion lieutenant said. "Only the teenage wolf and witch will be enrolled into the Academy. We came for them, so I suggest you step aside if you don't want any more trouble."

I wasn't crazy about his suggestion, so the lieutenant and I traded words, despite everyone gasping at the abusive heat and violent threats in the exchange, until the demigod intervened again.

"I'll spare your friends under one condition," he said with a bright, sexy, yet cruel smile, and my stupid heart fluttered.

I wasn't completely immune to him. After all, I was a human.

I leaned closer to hear his proposal. I would give him a chance to prove that not all demigods were inflexible tyrants who loved to stick absurd rules up their arrogant asses.

Dark pleasure flashed in his eyes, and he sniffed me again. I didn't draw back from him right away, despite my erratic heartbeat that warned me not to get too close or I'd get burned.

It seemed I had an effect on him, too. If my scent could muddle his mind, so be it.

But I didn't expect his scent of male, demigod, and sex to slam into my nostrils so potently. My mind went blank for a second.

I rectified my mistake by putting distance between us.

This wasn't the time to get screwed. I had two underage charges to protect.

I arched an eyebrow to show him that I'd walk if I didn't like the deal.

"And what is your condition, demigod?" I asked carefully.

"You go in their places, Marigold," the demigod purred.

CHAPTER 3

"Absolutely not!" Circe and Jasper jumped up from kneeling as if they'd just woken from a bad dream.

"It'll be the death of you, Marigold," Jasper objected fiercely. He had shifted back to a teenage boy and put on his tattered trousers. "You know that only those who have strong gods' blood in them can survive the trial in the Half-Blood Academy. Don't do this. We'll just go with them. It's no big deal."

It *was* a big deal. They were still too young to understand what they would walk into.

"Don't throw away your life for us, Marigold." Circe nodded. "We'll go with them. We aren't your responsibility anymore."

My heart sank; she sounded like she actually wanted to go. The way she gazed upon the demigod was like a teenager with a crush on her idol. But I'd thought she was into Jasper. My witch friend could be a bit fickle.

The demigod gave my team a stern look of warning, and both Circe and Jasper recoiled.

Jasper's opposition resonated with me. I wasn't as big a fool as the demigod thought.

"I won't go with you," I said, fixing my stare on the demigod. "I'm merely a human. I'm nothing special, so I won't survive the trial. You don't want my death on your conscience and my blood on your hands."

I paused for a second, not sure if he had a conscience. As one of the demigods who commanded Earth's war, I doubted he'd mind one more drop of blood on his hands. But I had to try to make him see reason. Maybe he would have a soft heart today.

"As you can see, my teammates are but an ordinary shifter and a mediocre witch," I offered. I had to hurt their feelings now and explain later. "I've lived with them for three years. I swear that they don't have gods' blood in their veins. If you force them to go through the trial, they'll die, too." The demigod leaned closer to me to listen, so I batted my eyelashes. "Man, please just let us go and take the punk werewolves with you. I'll be forever grateful. To show my gratitude, I'll send you a postcard every Christmas. And may God bless you."

So, yeah, we didn't celebrate Christmas anymore, but I'd given him my word, so I wouldn't correct it.

"The Half-Blood Academy is only for the descendants of the gods," the lieutenant cut in harshly. "It's a privilege to even be summoned. Your friends won't have a chance to get near the main campus. They'll go to the Other Academy, where supernaturals attend. There's no trial for non-descendants. When they graduate, they'll assist the Dominions." He eyed me, flashing a vengeful smirk. "As for you, if you go in their places, you won't be enrolled to the Other Academy. You'll take the magic trial in the Half-Blood Academy."

"Enough, Cameron," the demigod hissed.

He didn't want me to back out, and the Dominions couldn't force a human to take the Trial of the Blood Runes, which was solely reserved for the special race.

"I apologize for speaking out of turn, Demigod Axel," Cameron said.

My heart skipped a beat. So the demigod was the son of the bloodthirsty God of War. He must be bloodthirsty, too.

Was that why he wanted me in the Academy, to watch the blood runes bleed me dry?

"Your choice, Marigold," Axel said, my name rolling off his tongue sensually.

So I tossed out my last card.

"One technical problem, though," I said, raising a finger to emphasize my statement. "Your second-in-charge said those rogue werewolves are too old to attend the Academy. All three of us are too old for your school as well."

"How old are you?" he asked, considering me curiously, as if age was a big, inconvenient factor he could be swayed by.

Hope sparked in me. I lifted my chin. "I might look young, but I'm going on thirty. My friends are only a year or two younger. We're all heading to middle age soon. Very soon."

The lieutenant chuckled. "Nice try."

Axel nodded at me in approval. "That's the perfect age."

"What?" I cried, widening my eyes in dismay. "You're a demigod. You're an immortal. You don't understand that for a human, thirty is considered old, at least too old for any academy!"

"No more excuses, Marigold," Axel said firmly, his formerly amiable demeanor gone. "We've wasted enough time here. You're going with us."

Cameron snickered in unforgiving glee.

I'd booted him in the chest, and now he wanted to see my agonizing death in the trial.

~

The Dominions were going to get the deal of buy-one-get-two-free.

Jasper and Circe wouldn't leave me, even though I'd bought them both a free ticket to stay in Crack.

Circe was actually eager to attend an academy. The delighted glint in her eyes dimmed a little when she learned that she couldn't go to the Half-Blood Academy, but then they brightened again when Cameron told her that the two academies shared part of the campus with different classes, buildings, and training fields.

I understood that she desired to see the world and wanted to have more options in the future. A life in Crack wasn't much, but at least here we were free. But a seventeen-year old might not think like me. She'd wanted to step out of my shadow—though I'd never intended to overshadow her—especially during these last few months when she had grown more powerful. I should have seen the signs more clearly. She'd rolled her eyes at my orders ever since she'd started to regard me less as a mentor and more as her competition.

Circe had always been more ambitious than Jasper and me. I totally got it, but it didn't mean I didn't feel hurt. For three years I'd built this life with them, thinking we would always be together, like a family.

For a second, I almost regretted that I'd developed such attachment to both Jasper and Circe. It was tearing me apart to separate from them.

I should have learned my lesson when Vi had abandoned me.

Now that both Jasper and Circe had signed up, going to the Other Academy willingly, I could actually stay back, but it wasn't in me to just abandon them to the devices of the Dominions.

I'd have to see this through, to make sure that they would settle safely and well in the new school. The panic had left me when I'd learned that they weren't required to go through the blood rune trials.

Jasper laid a hand on my shoulder, as if reading my thoughts of turmoil. He'd always understood me. He'd always been in my corner, guarding me.

"Stay, Marigold," he said. "Don't throw your life away for us. It's time to think of yourself. Think what you really want. Please do this for me. If you go, you'll die at the trial, and you should know what it will do to me. If you die, it'll break me, and I won't be whole again. Please, I promise to come back to you when I can."

My eyes widened in surprise. Jasper had never been so open and emotional before. It didn't matter to him where he went, and he was willing to go to the Academy for me.

Maybe he was right. Maybe I should think of myself for once.

It made no sense now that both Jasper and Circe were going to the Other Academy and I would head to my own death at the trial. I held his warm, brown gaze, and an understanding passed between us.

I needed to bail out to preserve myself. I wouldn't be going to the Half-Death Academy anymore.

A sudden wild wind reeled between us, throwing Jasper away from me, and then the demigod was in my face.

"What's that for?" I hissed. "I was just saying goodbye to my team. I don't think I'll be going to your Half-Blood Academy." I added bitterly, "You've gotten what you came for. You don't get to have all three of us."

Anger swirled in Axel's dark amber eyes.

"A Dominion soldier is made of tough material," he growled. "You don't just go back on your word."

"My words were based on me going in the place of my team," I retorted. "Since they're both going anyway, the condition is nullified. I'm not stupid enough to throw myself at your trial for no reason and then die. Plus, I'm not a

Dominion soldier. I'm merely a human who doesn't have an ounce of gods' blood in me."

"I'm not so sure about that," he said. "We'll test if you're powerful enough to survive the trial. Words are binding. I'm a Demigod of War." At his declaration, he grew bigger and taller, his leather coat billowing in the wind he created, and everyone, except me, recoiled from his display of pure, terrifying power.

I wasn't affected by his magic, probably because I was furious and busy glaring at him, so I resisted his power again, just like before.

"I won't allow you to go back on your word, Marigold," he confirmed, "and set a bad example for other soldiers. The contract is nullified only when I say so. And I say you'll go through the trial and attend the Academy."

He didn't care that the trial would be the death of me, he was so insistent on proving a point and sticking to the rule he'd just made up.

It was obvious that no matter what I could say, plead, or beg, the demigod wouldn't let me off the hook, even if he had to drag me to Half-Death Academy with his bare hands.

"Fuck you!" I said. "My life means nothing to you, but it means something to me."

While he was distracted, seething that I had the temerity to curse a demigod, I kicked his knee hard.

I wanted to throw him off balance to give myself a small opening to flee. All I did was hurt my ankle at the brutal force I'd used. Booting his knee was like kicking iron pilings.

No matter, I broke into a dead run. My whole life, no one had ever run faster than me, so I should be able to get away. Without Jasper and Circe as a responsibility anymore, I didn't slow down for them or anyone.

I zoomed between the buildings like a flash, turned a corner, and shot toward the forest. I couldn't go home to the library since I wasn't confident that the ward could keep a demigod out.

The forest would be my best bet.

There were a host of monsters inside. If he followed me into territory that was unfamiliar to him, the monsters could attack him and help shake him off my trail.

I didn't see anyone behind me when I reached the edge of the forest, so I spared a moment to grin, ready to charge into the forest and hide in the high, thick canopy.

A force dragged me back, then a strong arm snaked around my waist in an iron grip.

"What the fu—?" I cried.

I kicked, trying to struggle free, but to no avail. Then a whirlwind sucked me in, spinning me until I couldn't see straight.

When my dizziness faded, I was standing before a black van with the sliding side door open. Axel still clutched me firmly, his arm around my midsection.

The demigod had just teleported me.

No wonder he hadn't bothered to chase me when I burst into a run. The fucker had been content to let me suffer from tight air burning in my lungs before he whizzed in to snatch me.

My eyes lit with rage at the humiliation of being captured so easily, yet I noticed a woman soldier, the only female in the Dominion asshole team, looking at me in envy.

What? She envied that the demigod had kidnapped me?

"Strip off her weapons," Axel ordered.

"Don't you dare have your men touch me!" I hissed.

"No men will be allowed to touch you, minx," Axel said, his voice harsh and possessive. "Marie will remove your weapons. You've proven to be a menace, and we can't afford for you to cause more trouble on the road whenever I'm not around to stop you."

"I'm not a troublemaker," I said.

Axel shrugged, not convinced.

While he held me, pinning me down, the female soldier came forward to extract the spear from my hand, the bow and quiver of arrows from my back and shoulders, a pocket knife from my sleeve, a few hidden daggers from my boots, my pants, and several other weapons from inside my leather jacket.

The soldiers around us gasped at the number of weapons I carried.

"You missed one, Marie," Axel informed the soldier as he pulled a silver needle from my hair.

Cameron whistled. "She'll fit right in with us."

He'd hated my guts a few minutes ago.

I hissed, "I don't share your confidence much."

A couple of soldiers chuckled, either at my humiliation or my daring, I wasn't sure.

Axel frowned at me. "Why did you need that many weapons, Marigold?"

"A girl shouldn't be faulted for trying to take care of herself," I said, surveying our surroundings. We were on the side of the road with five soldiers around a van, which meant the other two must be with Circe and Jasper.

"Where's my team?" I asked.

"They're no longer your team," Axel said. "They're in the other van, heading to the Other Academy now."

He scooped me up, and involuntarily, I clasped my hands behind his neck. My body purred. He grinned, and I realized my mistake. Releasing my arms from around him, I pondered if I should elbow him in the throat.

He should have a weakness, right? And the throat might just be it.

He put me down on the back seat of the van and buckled me in with the safety belt.

I wiggled on the leather seat as I suddenly got a bright idea. "I think you made a mistake by separating my team and me."

He squinted, yet his hands still held my waist. "I don't make mistakes."

"Listen," I said, giving him a smile for the first time since we'd fought and he'd captured me. "I don't have a trace of gods' blood in me. I'm actually a witch. I'm sorry for hiding that part of my heritage from you. Being a witch, I should go to the Other Academy."

I could survive the Other Academy. I'd just borrow some of the spells Circe created and toss them here and there. I'd pretend to be a witch as long as I could so I would see Jasper and Circe settle down and watch over them for a little while before I got kicked out.

Or when the Dominions weren't looking or lost interest in me, I'd slip away, alone, if my team chose this new life for themselves.

My heart broke a little at the thought of moving on, but that was how things were now.

I'd be a free agent again, but I might have to leave Crack behind.

The Dominions would never find me again.

"Give up already," Cameron said. "If you were a witch, we'd have known. Our psychic ball showed only your two pack members. You aren't on any chart of any map." At Axel's glare, he clamped his mouth shut.

"Behave, Marigold," the demigod said, giving me a measured look before his lingering hands left my body. A secret, treacherous part of me screamed at the absence of his heat and touch.

"Your friends will be better off in the Other Academy," he continued. "They'll get an education and regular meals and will be with their own kinds."

I swallowed as I had to admit the truth of his words, no matter how hard it was for me to let go of my team and let them choose what they really wanted for their own lives. This could be a better opportunity for them.

Just when I starting warming up to his comfort, he added, "So will you." As if he believed I'd survive the trial. But the next sentence out of his sensual, cruel mouth made me hate him again. "But if you give my soldiers any more headaches on the road, the other team will take it out on your friends."

I stiffened, enraged at his callous threat, a threat aimed at the only two people I cared about in this world. But before I could come up with a vicious comeback for his ruthless coercion, the demigod ducked his head out of the van, and then he was gone.

There was nothing I could do but go along with this travesty—for now, anyway. I bit my nail as the van lurched forward, musing over how I was going to survive the trial.

CHAPTER 4

The armored van sped through Crack, a "wild west" neither the demons nor the demigods had ever graced with their presence until this unfortunate day in Crack's history.

The glinting metal on top of the library, my old home, soon disappeared from view.

The Dominions hadn't allowed us to pick up our personal stuff.

"We must get to our regiment before sunset," Cameron said with an uncompromising look.

I kind of got it. Demons were more powerful when the sun went down; intense light weakened them. The Dominions didn't want to get hit on the road.

As I'd said, half of Earth belonged to Lucifer and the other half belonged to the gods—specifically Ares, the God of War. The four demigods helped Ares run the show on their patches of land while four archdemons served the devil on theirs.

It was like a pissing contest between the war god and the devil.

It was funny how Lucifer and Ares had divided the globe. They didn't split it in the middle. They'd carved up every state and every city in half, leaving some regions as neutral zones.

It was almost like they had cut a dirty deal—or were playing a game and had divided the board up evenly to start.

And they kept fighting to gain more territories and control Earth's main resources.

In New York state where we lived, north belonged to the gods, and south was the devil's. In New York City, Queens and the Bronx were the demons' territory while Brooklyn and Staten Island were the demigods' domain. Manhattan was a neutral zone, where fights broke out every day.

I sighed. I should worry more about myself than the demigods and demons.

Marie, the female Dominion soldier who had stripped me of every weapon, sat on my right and a tattooed soldier on my left with me sandwiched between them as if they thought I'd still try to escape while the car was running.

Another soldier perched on the seat behind me.

Must Axel put five soldiers with me while leaving only two with Circe and Jasper? What if the other van got attacked by demons while we raced down the highway?

"Where is Axel?" I asked. "Shouldn't he escort the vans and keep us safe?"

Even though I knew there were no good guys, I'd rather be in the hands of the Dominion of the Gods than in the claws of the demons. My early encounter with that demon had left a chill in my bones.

To be possessed by a demon was even worse than being eaten alive.

"Babysitting isn't in a demigod's job description," Cameron said from the passenger seat. His pose remained alert, as if he expected to go into battle at any moment. "Better drill that into your head now, in case you ever become a Dominion soldier."

"I also recommended you not poke your nose into the demigod's business, fledgling," Marie snorted, "if you know what's good for you. You've riled up the Demigod of War enough today. If he rode with you in this van, he might have to strangle you before we reach the Academy. Demigod Axel is more bloodthirsty than his older brethren. It's a wonder he hasn't squashed you yet, given your attitude. A human life is nothing to a demigod. Axel has killed for lesser offenses."

She gave me another once-over. "I don't think it's your face he's interested in." I could see her point since my face was covered by soot and dirt. "Beauty is a dime a dozen at the Academy, since anyone with an ounce of god's blood is easy on the eyes. There're plenty of gorgeous women fighting to get the attention of the demigods, and you don't exactly make the cut since I don't think you're one of us. You're something else. I guess that's why Demigod Axel was obsessed with bringing you to the Academy to see if you can survive the merciless ritual." She sent me one last pitiful glance. "I don't think you'll pass."

I was heading to my death because of that asshole's sick game.

I didn't retort despite her derision. I needed more intel on the demigods, the Academy, and most importantly, the Ritual of the Blood Runes.

I arched an eyebrow at her, hoping to goad her into talking more. "Oh yeah, you think?"

"With her brazen spirit, she might just pass," Cameron chimed in. "She's the first creature I've ever seen who isn't afraid of Demigod Axel. Did you see how she resisted his power, as no mortal could ever do?" He turned halfway to peek at me over his broad shoulder. "If you pass the trial, you can join my team. I can probably use someone like you, but you must drop that bad attitude of yours."

This time I snorted. "I don't have a bad attitude, and I'm not a follower. I take shit from no one."

"Bah!" Marie said. "They'll break you, and I'll be there to watch instead of catch you."

"Thank you," I said in mocking gratitude. "You're such a good friend."

Suddenly, Cameron poked his head out the window, then flung his hand backward. Lightning shot out at a truck that had nearly rammed into the rear of the van.

The truck flapped up into the air and then plummeted to the ground. The entire highway shook like we were in an earthquake.

Our driver floored the gas pedal at the same time as Cameron's attack, so our van was at the edge of the shockwave.

The next second, the van bumped an armored car in the right lane.

Marie moved to the left window, rolled it half down, and blasted bullets into three motorcycles approaching from behind us.

I had damn fast reflexes, yet I'd missed how a lightweight machine gun had appeared in her hands. The

Dominions weren't fools. While conversing with me, they'd stayed vigilant for any looming danger and reacted super fast.

The rest of the soldiers also moved into seamless action.

Bullets, lightning, spells, and fire exchanged between the Dominions and our attackers. Two of the motorcycles were tossed into the air by a soldier's magic and Marie's bullets, but more enemy forces were coming.

Cameron kept throwing lightning with a wicked grin on his face. He ducked back into the van every now and then to avoid the spell fires and the bullets that ricocheted off the armored body of the van.

The lieutenant was a descendant of Zeus, the God of Sky.

Luckily, he hadn't thrown lightning at me when we'd fought.

I didn't see the other van that held Circe and Jasper. They had less manpower, and my stomach twisted in worry for them.

The asshole demigod shouldn't have separated my team from me.

"Give me a weapon," I shouted. "I'm not going to be a sitting duck here."

"Just sit tight and enjoy the show," Cameron said while tossing another lightning bolt at a new car that chased us.

"You can't just throw those fancy bolts of yours all day, can you?" I asked, planning to steal a firearm from either Marie or the soldier on my other side.

"Nope," Cameron said, producing a shotgun and firing it with one hand. "You think I'm a god?"

"You're obviously very far from a god," I said.

Another enemy automobile slammed into a civilian vehicle after being hit by Cameron's merciless bullets plus lightning bolts.

Our van sped onto a bridge made of steel, concrete, and cables. To my surprise, the attacks stopped abruptly.

"Why didn't they follow?" I asked.

"We've reached our territory," said the soldier on my other side. "This is the Verrazano-Narrows Bridge. In case you don't know, Half-Blood Academy is on Staten Island."

"Thank you," I said. "That's very informative."

He chuckled. In addition to tattoos, he had a diamond stud in his left earlobe.

"Could you check my friends' statuses in the other van, Cameron?" I asked.

"You think I take orders from you now?" Cameron snorted.

"Please," I said. "I need to know that they're safe."

"The other van wasn't attacked," Cameron said. "It seems trouble follows only you. You know what? I changed my mind. Even if you survive the trial, I don't want you on my team. You're more trouble than you're worth. Sticking around you for too long, you might get us all killed."

"Thank you for the confidence," I said.

Marie nodded in agreement. "We've never had an incident rounding up descendants until you. And none of the demigods ever supervised a recruit mission before."

"I'm not bad luck," I shouted. "I'm an asset. I took out several criminal lords and gangs in Crack when I was a few years younger."

The soldiers traded an unconvinced look.

"You might not be the worst luck to yourself," Marie concluded, "but you are to others, like the criminal lords."

"I protect the innocent," I protested. Like Jasper and Circe.

In no time, we crossed the bay and reached the other end of the bridge.

Soldiers wearing Dominion badges were posted at all the checkpoints. There were even air patrols above the lush, green island.

No one stopped us, and our driver no longer raced like a maniac.

Security seemed air-tight as I spotted heavily-armed soldiers on every few blocks on the island.

We passed by streets, buildings, stores, and a large park, which all looked nice. The demigod-controlled Staten Island hadn't been tainted by the war between the gods and demons. This was probably what the old civilization had looked like before both types of assholes invaded our world.

The van cruised through a vast gate as it slid open from the middle. Etched into the left side of the reinforced red wall, giant letters of gold proclaimed this to be Half-Blood Academy. On the right wall, the school crest displayed an eagle above the waves piercing a lightning bolt with a blade that also looked like a key connecting the sky and ocean.

The eagle was the power sign for the God of War, the lightning bolt was the God of Sky's birthright, the ocean was the God of Sea's domain, and the blade was the Sword of Hades and Key to the Underworld.

The four demigods were the only direct descendants of Ares, Zeus, Poseidon, and Hades, and thus this military school was named the Half-Blood Academy. I wondered if I would meet the rest of the demigods before I either survived or perished in the ritual.

Armed soldiers waved for the van to roll ahead as they recognized everyone, except me, in the van. They probably didn't regard me as much of a threat.

As soon as the van braked at the circular driveway in front of the main campus, its door opened with a sharp metal sound, spitting out half of the team.

They lined up on either side of the vehicle, waiting for me to let myself out.

I leapt out of the van, squinting as I surveyed the campus: a gem-like pond, lush gardens, century-old trees.

I was surprised at how vast this place was.

The skyscrapers were so modern with steel and glass, the old stone buildings had elaborate carvings that spoke of rich tradition and history, and the low-rise structures were in a Victorian style.

Several vans parked around the circle.

Suddenly I caught sight of Jasper and Circe at the far end of the square.

Jasper darted his worried gaze around the crowd, as if searching for me. Circe looked so thrilled at this new environment that she twirled in a small dance. My breath hitched in my throat. She was young. She had no idea what kind of tough life lay ahead.

It wasn't dancing and parties and boys, for sure.

Now that we were inside this fence, we'd never have freedom, not unless we escaped.

"Jas, Circe!" I called, bolting toward them, but two of the soldiers who'd escorted me immediately blocked my path.

Marie dragged me back.

"What the fuck are you doing?" I said. "I need to see my friends!"

"I'm doing you a favor, girl," Marie said. "I'm helping you survive in this place."

"Demigod Axel has ordered that if you cause trouble, your friends will suffer the consequences," Cameron said. "Do you copy?"

I glared at him, shaking in anger. He held my gaze, daring me punch him with my tight fists. He'd punch back, then probably shock me good with his lightning.

"You need to focus on your trial, Marigold," Marie said, softening her tone. "If you live, you'll get to see them once every three weeks in the main dining hall where all the students and trainers socialize. Your friends belong to the Other Academy on the secondary campus, a place for all other supernaturals, like witches, shifters, warlocks, mages, fae, and vampires."

"But shouldn't my friends be here for me during the trial?" I said in a last-ditch effort to get the Dominions to show a little sympathy or bend a little. "Could you talk to Axel about it, please?"

Marie snorted. "He'd have my head for calling him for something like that. Look, rules are rules. The Ritual of Blood Runes is only to be observed by the demigods, the senior Dominion officers, and other initiates. Outsiders, not even the leaders of the supernaturals who aren't descendants of the gods, are not allowed to watch."

"I just want to see my team one last time before shit goes down," I said. "If I don't make it, at least I get to say goodbye."

"Then you make sure you make it," Marie said.

There was no point in arguing with her. She knew it wasn't up to me but the gods' power that decided who lived and who was doomed.

I stared into empty space. I didn't want to ruin the first day for Jasper and Circe in their academy life.

My shoulders sagged as I watched the soldiers take my former teammates down the opposite path and vanish behind a building trellised with ivy and lilac.

That might be the last of them I ever saw.

CHAPTER 5

I joined twelve other candidates, some of them a little younger and some a little older than me. I bathed and put on a white robe, the only thing they offered me.

I was so sick and tired of fighting the Dominions and ending up nowhere, so I didn't even bother to complain that I didn't get to wear a bra and panties.

In low spirits and bare feet, I padded quietly down the cobbled path lined with red maple trees along with other initiates.

They had arrived a week earlier and already formed a clique. Six of them gathered around Demetra and Jack, hanging on their every word. The other four were outsiders like me.

Two of the outcasts constantly darted longing gazes at the popular group, as if that would get them into the exclusive club. All they got was the evil eye from the snobs, who regarded the rest of us as the slough beneath their noble feet.

"Stay away!" A clique girl, Barbara, hissed and patted her sleeve as if even our gazes could dirty her clothes.

The instructor had read all our names when he brought us here, and I'd made a point of learning them.

The other two outsiders, Nat and Yelena, acted like childhood friends, which was probably why they didn't seem to care much about being shunned.

I didn't give a damn who was more or less popular either.

Even though we were all dressed in the same white robes, it was easy to detect who came from an affluent family and who was raised in poverty.

I had my own rough-around-the-edges style, which I'd seen some guys use to their social advantage when they owned it. The bad boy appeal, I guess, it didn't work so well for me.

Class existed everywhere, and wherever you went, you could never avoid bitches and dicks.

That Demetra chick had been bragging about her revered family non-stop, and her high-pitched voice began to grate on my thin nerves. Man, I was brooding on a survival strategy here.

"The invitation came as expected." She started again. "Obviously, the demigods know that I'm a quarter, which is a big deal. They must have looked into my family's legacy. None of the academies has had a quarter in nearly a century. I was born to rise above all others and sit next to the demigods."

"I heard that the demigods are all super hot," Barbara whispered, licking her lips, her eyes sparking with hope. "They can have anyone they want."

My damn super hearing could catch every word.

"Believe me, now that I'm here, they won't look anywhere else," Demetra declared with one hundred percent confidence.

The other girls looked at her with equal measures of envy and admiration.

From eavesdropping on their gossip, I realized that no one, except me, had resisted being recruited by the Dominions. Most people considered it a privilege to be summoned by the Half-Blood Academy.

Once initiates passed the trials, they were verified as descendants of the gods. Their elite status would enhance their family's names and influence.

I was probably the only one who didn't give a damn about being elite.

"We're the best the world has to offer," Demetra said while she thrust her chin toward mostly me. "I'm not sure the rest will make the cut. There're always winners, and there're always losers. The Academy can't have the weak among us. It's a great practice to weed them out."

Did she even have a brain?

I'd had enough of her shit talking.

"Can we have some quiet before the ritual," I asked as politely as I could. "Please, ladies and gentlemen?"

The clique gasped at my audacity to even talk to them, as my low class status seemed to mean I was supposed to shut up and bow down.

Yelena and Nat gave me a curious glance, and the other two timid outsiders held their breath, as if expecting lightning to strike me now. They even pulled back a little farther from me to show the clique that we weren't in league.

Walking ahead of me at two o'clock, Demetra snapped her golden head around and spared me a contemptuous glance over her shoulder.

"Are you the lowly girl who talked to *me*?" she asked incredulously, apparently not believing that I dared talk to a "queen" without kneeling or whatever sucking up she was used to. Her gorgeous face twisted into a sneer.

"Lowly?" I asked huskily. "Wow, that's classy. So, you're the self-appointed queen bee who lives in her own delusions of grandeur? Pardon if I don't curtsy. I've never learned to be submissive. I don't curtsy to the demigods. What makes you think I'd even nod my head to you?"

Her minions gasped, as if they had collective hiccups.

"How rude," one of the girls said in a polished accent. "The low class hussy never learned manners."

"Then show me your manners," I said. "They probably come from where the sun doesn't shine."

"Don't mind her," a clique boy said dismissively. "She isn't worth it. She just wants attention, and we're not going to give it to her."

I shook my head and laughed. "Comedians."

Jack, the boy leader of the clique, turned his narrowed, hazel eyes on me from beside Demetra. He was the largest among us, and he had this tough build and look, like he could kill anyone without a peep from his conscience, despite his handsome face.

He appeared at ease and totally fit in. He might turn out even stronger than Cameron.

Speaking of, Cameron emerged in a new, clean uniform with the three-bar ranking on his badge. He strode beside me.

Jack dimmed his death-threat look and kept walking.

Demetra immediately noticed the Dominion lieutenant and flashed him a saccharine smile, the voltage so high it could melt most guys' belts off their trousers.

I hated to admit it, but she had looks going for her with her perfectly toned body. And lucky for her, blonde was still in fashion. Maybe it always would be. She could've been a successful runway model if she hadn't come to the Academy.

She evidently knew it, too. I bet she'd use her stunning looks as her most lethal weapon in any setting. That vain confidence was why she openly boasted that once she'd caught the demigods' eyes, they'd never wander again. If she could sink her claws into one of them, or all of them for all I cared, she could have offspring with a demigod. Then she could brag to no end that her children were a step closer to being demigods themselves.

What a wonderful plan!

Only if she didn't open her mouth again and spew more haughty nonsense.

But then most guys didn't care, as long as they got to sleep with a bimbo like her.

"You couldn't even dye your hair properly, harpy," Demetra scoffed. "Can't afford a salon?"

"For your information, queen bee," I said. "My hair color is natural. No offense, but you might need to get your eyes checked, or I doubt the Dominions will accept you into their *elite* ranks."

"Really, Marigold?" Cameron said, grinning at me. "Your hair is natural? No kidding. I agree with the other girl. I don't think you dyed it properly."

He still held a grudge against me, probably because I'd booted him in the chest during our encounter, or more likely I'd hurt his feelings by turning down his offer of recruiting me for his team should I pass the ritual.

Demetra giggled, flicking her long blonde hair like a supermodel in appreciation of Cameron's support and her own irresistible charm.

Who was I kidding? She held quite an ambition to take on the demigods and get at least one of them to have babies with her.

"You're one to talk, lieutenant," I snorted. "I expected better from you."

"Stop pouting, Marigold," Cameron continued. "It isn't befitting an initiate to have that sour expression sitting on your face. Man up and be the soldier you were born to be."

"I'm not a man," I said. "So I don't need to man up. And I wasn't born to be a soldier under your thumb."

"I can't tell which gender you belong to," he said.

The clique snickered, and Demetra giggled in an annoyingly high pitch.

Nat and Yelena threw me a sympathetic look. Everyone knew it was a bad business to get on the bad side of a Dominion, let alone an officer.

"Thanks, man," I said to Cameron. "Look what you brought me into—a puberty drama, as if I need that shit on top of my other shit piles."

"You brought yourself into that shit pile," he said. "I'm only surprised that you refuse to appreciate us for saving you from an unproductive, wasted life."

Now that irked me, and I became prickly as a hedgehog. "You Dominions forced me to leave my home and my team behind to come here. You took the good life away from me."

"What kind of good life are we talking about, Marigold?" Marie from the van chimed in curiously, popping up near me.

Some of the clique appeared surprised and unhappy. The Dominion officers probably didn't associate much with the initiates, even though these two were merely taunting and ridiculing me.

I hadn't seen Marie since I was sent to the public bath chamber to have my one-minute shower. To my frustration, after I exited the stall I found that someone had taken away all my outfits and left me with only a robe.

I gave the Dominion soldier a glare, "A life of freedom." I flapped the hem of the robe. "Not this life of wearing a robe without panties. They didn't even leave a G-String, for gods' sakes."

If Marie had been there, I think she'd have the courtesy to find me underwear. I sensed she might actually like me.

Marie howled with laughter, and several escorting soldiers joined in, sending me glances as if they hadn't seen me before.

The clique screwed up their facial expressions to show they were disgusted by my vulgarity.

"What?" I asked both Cameron and Marie. "No one has ever complained about this inhumane, no underwear treatment?"

"Nope," Cameron deadpanned. "All, except you, considered it a privilege."

"Pardon me," I glared at him incredulously. "What if someone laughed so hard they peed a little?"

Or scared the literal shit out of themselves in the middle of the ritual.

"Stop! Marigold," Marie wiped a teardrop, then another, from the corner of her eyes. "Just stop."

In the background, Jack made a sniffing sound. I hoped he didn't smell a whiff of pee.

"That rogue doesn't smell like us," he said, his tone positive. "I don't think she's a descendant. She won't make it."

"Jack has the magical ability to sense and detect the descendants of gods," Demetra declared, gloating.

My heart froze as her statement hit me right in the bull's eye. While the rest of the initiates walked to their glory, this might be a death walk for me.

I scanned the tight security around us and realized I'd have to take a chance with the ritual, if I didn't want to be put down within seven feet.

"Then why is she even among us?" asked a clique boy with distaste.

"That harpy must want to take a chance," Demetra explained, as if she knew everything about me, "since this is her only opportunity to rise above her pathetic status. A low class girl like her will do anything to move up the social ladder, though they all gamble and lose." She made a disgusted sound with her nose. "I wonder how many soldiers she opened her legs for to get here. So sad because no matter how wide her legs spread, it won't—"

I lunged at her, grabbing a handful of her blonde hair and pulling hard. She screamed as she stumbled back and struggled to break free. Jack charged at me, but Cameron and Marie stepped between us first.

The Dominions pried my fingers off Demetra's hair, dragged me back, and pinned me in place. The other Dominion soldiers barked orders at the group, urging them to keep walking.

None of them wanted to attract a demigod's attention.

I wasn't proud of myself for pulling hair—I was more of a punch-you-in-the-teeth kind of girl. But I was too mad to care about my dignity or anyone else's. The whole day's frustration and the fear of what was coming all accumulated and accelerated.

Plus, when I faced bullies, I became an aggressor myself.

I took no shit, and walking toward death's door wasn't going to change my attitude either.

"I don't give a fuck how thick a god's blood is in your nasty veins," I warned, not even struggling in Cameron's and Marie's grips. "Talk shit like that again, and I'll beat the crap out of you."

"You're dead, you inferior human!" Demetra shrieked. "You don't have an ounce of any god's DNA in you. You should never have come here. You won't come out of that building alive. You'll suffer an agonizing death before the first rune—"

"What the hell is going on here?" a voice boomed, carrying potent magic.

Axel appeared at the top of the stairs we were about to climb, which led toward a magnificent yet intimidating red building.

Power rolled off him in an icy wind, crushing down everything and everyone in its path.

As one, everyone dropped to their knees, except for me, again.

Even the noises of the wind hushed.

The Dominion soldiers around us quickly straightened their outfits, which were already straight and spotless.

"Are you causing trouble again, Marigold?" Axel asked impatiently.

"Who? Me?" I asked darting my eyes around in innocent confusion.

"What did I say about the consequences of you not behaving?" he pursued.

I bit my lip. He'd let his Dominions punish Jasper and Circe. "This damn robe is uncomfortable," I said.

His dark amber eyes dipped to my robe before roving across my every inch.

Maybe I shouldn't have complained about my wardrobe. I suddenly understood what it meant to be caressed without touching.

The demigod could undress me with his mere smoldering gaze, and wearing nothing but a robe didn't help. If I had on my hunter attire, I'd be in my element and know how to deal with him.

Right now, I'd never felt more vulnerable than under the weight of his blunt, heated, and assessing gaze.

Worse, a swirl of liquid fire licked the flesh between my thighs, and my sex became slick and wet.

My face burned. Goddammit! What had I said about not wearing panties?

Gods help me if my lady bits got any wetter!

I lifted my chin, staring back at the demigod in defiance as I tightened the front of my robe.

An amused, wicked, and possessive smile ghosted his lips before it disappeared as if it had never been there.

"You were out of my sight for only a few hours," Axel sighed, "and you're already causing chaos. I'm starting to wonder if it was worth it to bring you here."

My eyes sparkled in hope, and I stepped toward him without his invitation, though he was still twenty stairs away from me. "You'll let me go?"

He regarded me darkly, seeming to think about it, and I smiled at him in order to get in his good graces.

"Nope," he said, his face turning hard. "You *will* go through the trial, Marigold, even if I have to drag you through it myself."

A wild wind rolled down from the stairs, shuffling my robe and caressing the valley between my thighs. I parted my lips and widened my eyes at the sensation. Then the naughty wind was gone, as was the infuriating Demigod of War.

Demetra snickered as she rose to her feet. She must believe that Axel was using the ritual as a means to humiliate, punish, and execute me.

She would be the cheerleader for that, wouldn't she?

But she might be right, though.

I refused to let any of them further crush my spirit.

I paused at the base of the stairs and turned to Marie. "May I borrow your boots, Marie?" I asked. At least I could try to improve my current condition as the first step. "You have socks. My bare feet are fragile. It really hurt walking on that long, cobbled path." I raised my head and peeked at the cobbled stairs leading to the red building where the ritual would be held and lives would be lost.

Maybe I was stalling. I had no courage left. "Man, just look at those stairs. I don't think my feet, which aren't made of stones, can take it anymore."

The clique shot me dirty looks and climbed the stairs with vigor. The other two outsiders followed closely behind them, showing their strength as well.

Nat and Yelena paused beside me.

"C'mon, Marigold," Yelena offered. "Let's go. You can lean on Nat and me."

"Get moving, Marigold," Cameron said, his voice back to harsh and threatening. "You nearly got my rank stripped with that hair-dragging stunt. No more hassles, or you'll be very sorry."

I started to wonder if he had bipolar disorder.

"And the answer to lending you my boots is a big no." Marie chuckled. "Your feet are the least of your concerns now. You don't want to keep getting on the bad side of the demigods."

I sighed in dismay as I climbed the stairs with Yelena and Nat. We were the last row. I could no longer stall.

"Even if the ritual doesn't kill me," I murmured to myself, "someone here will murder me eventually."

"You bet," Cameron said. "If you don't keep your mouth shut."

We reached the top of the stairs. The ritual building's steel and glass double doors opened in invitation.

I took a deep breath and stepped through the door, the famous phrase echoing chillingly in the back chambers of my head. *Lasciate ogne speranza, voi ch'intrate.*

Abandon all hope, **ye** who enter here.

CHAPTER 6

The Hall of Olympia was the most majestic place I'd ever seen. Man, even the columns were made of gold. The high ceilings were painted with murals depicting the war of the gods.

Didn't they say that the winners wrote history?

Twelve Olympian gods' statues stood close to the four walls, surrounding us. On the rising dais sat one large throne flanked by four smaller ones. All of them were adorned with rare gems, gold, and diamonds.

The biggest throne likely belonged to Ares, the God of War, who was leading Earth's army against Lucifer and his demon hordes. The rest of the thrones were there for the four demigods.

One could easily tell which throne belonged to which demigod by the symbols carved into each one's arms and high back.

Six initiates stood to the left side of the door, and the other six had been positioned on the right side with me. High-ranking Dominion officers lined up in two columns from the dais all the way to the door. A few elite students from the seniors, judging from their uniforms, were mixed into the ranks of the Dominion officers.

I bet they had already been selected as future leaders of Dominion of the Gods, which granted them the privilege of watching the show—seeing who lived and who died.

The initiates were as tense as me, but most of the clique looked more excited than anxious. They were the hounds on a blood trail, so confident of their godly heritage, no matter how distant it might be.

Demetra shot me several contemptuous glances, as if dying to tell me how much she looked forward to watching me embarrass myself in front of everyone before my painful death.

I glared back, of course.

Everyone had heard Jack's diagnosis of me being one hundred percent weak human. No one in this room believed I had enough gods' blood to survive this barbaric ritual.

Despite that, I tried to put up a brave façade, but the blood had drained from my face as soon as I'd stepped into the hall of death.

I studied the empty thrones.

Where were the demigods? Were they all going to observe the ritual? I'd seen Axel at the top of the stairs before he vanished thirty minutes ago. Where was he now? My thoughts darted from foreboding to how his magical caress had made me wet and how his power had called to me.

"Attention!" a deep male voice boomed, and I nearly jumped out of my skin.

For fuck's sake. Was it necessary to yell like that when the entire atrium was as quiet as a graveyard?

A tall man wearing a white priest robe stepped into the center of the hall with a flaming dagger. Crimson, gold, and black runes danced on the blade. The crimson ones looked very much like they'd been drawn in blood.

Holy fuck! Was he going to use that dagger on us?

No way. I was not okay with that.

The other initiates also widened their eyes.

If we all protested, they might stop the ritual. I scrutinized the other initiates for even a spark of rebellion. My shoulders sagged, in stark contrast to the others, who all stood tall and proud—even the four other outsiders. I'd be the only one standing up to the priest, and one voice would be easily and quickly smothered.

The priest's piercing silver eyes sparked with lightning as they swept over us, identifying him as a descendant of Zeus. The god's blood must be potent in him.

I sniffed. Yep, his power grade was like seven.

He fixed his flashing gaze on me a second longer than the others, and I wondered what I'd done wrong this time.

Uh, I was inhaling and judging his power. I instantly put on a blank mask. No one liked to be sniffed at, which typically implied you had an unpleasant odor or something.

The priest shifted his gaze away from me and glided a hand in the air like a conductor, as if to signal the first violinist to start the first notes. But there was no orchestra but us, the nervous bunch of initiates and the stone-faced, cold-hearted observers.

However, at his wave, an operating table of wood and steel materialized between him and us.

My throat tightened; my breath shortened.

Shit, the priest was going to get everyone to lie on the table one by one and cut them with the blade and see who could survive it.

Could I still run?

Anxiety shot through me, and I felt the urge to pee. Should I raise my hand and ask for permission to go to the bathroom first?

It might be my only chance to escape.

Just when I was about to shoot my hand up, intense wind and light twirled through the hall. Power charged the air, whipping it like living electricity. Water, too, made an appearance as humidity drenched the air, thick and heavy against my skin.

Then three giant figures materialized, each sitting upon a throne. Everyone's attention was glued to them, and the initiates' eyes went round with awe.

It wasn't merely the power rolling off the demigods in spades. They were the most gorgeous beings I'd ever seen. Each of them had the kind of perfect male physique men would die to attain—and women would die for a chance to ride—and I bet the demigods didn't even need weight training to maintain those hot vessels.

Even I felt a bit overwhelmed. Unlike the drooling initiates around me, though, my mind was too occupied with dread over the ritual to fully appreciate the demigods' masculine beauty.

When you were worried about your own mortality, lust had to take the backseat.

My gaze found Axel first since I'd had some kind of dealings with him already. His amber eyes focused on me.

He even winked at me good-naturedly as a strand of rich, brown hair dropped to his bright forehead.

I wasn't in the mood to wink back. I'd learned the hard way that getting the attention of a demigod was never a good thing.

I tore my livid gaze from him to regard the regal demigod perched on the throne of lightning. The Demigod of Sky had deep blue eyes and cropped golden hair that made him look more like a military god than the Demigod of War. Maybe Axel didn't like people to stereotype him, so he aimed for a casual, playboy style?

The Demigod of Sky had a red cape draped around him, and his silver and black armor highlighted every taut muscle and defined every ridge.

The lightning in his eyes was much more potent than that in the priest's eyes.

The sky demigod looked too delicious for his own good. Fine. Next.

My gaze drifted to the giant of a man who'd taken possession of the throne with the symbol of a trident protruding from seafoam on it.

The Demigod of the Sea.

Silver hair flowed down to his broad, armored shoulders. It looked so silky and smooth and shining that it made me wonder what kind of shampoo he'd been using. He might consider it blasphemy if I asked him about that, though.

The sea demigod looked every bit as sexy as his brethren, but there was something else about him I was wary of, even detested. I could sense his capricious nature and explosive temper, and I'd heard that he was the most vicious among all the demigods.

I categorized him as the super-villain type.

As if sensing my assessment, his cruel, seductive, and violet eyes trained on me. We locked gazes for a heartbeat, and menace flashed through his narrowed eyes. None of the initiates stared at the demigods as boldly as I did.

Why the hell not? They still had some humanity left, right?

And I liked to look freely. It wasn't just attitude—I was genuinely curious. I liked to think, evaluate, classify, and judge. What could he do to me and what harm could I do to him just by looking?

But the asshole sea demigod seemed to take serious offense anyway. His power assaulted me the next nanosecond. Waves of pressure crushed into me, kicking me in the gut, knocking brutally on my knees. He wanted to humiliate me and make me the only one to kneel before him in front of everyone.

Axel had tried and failed. I wouldn't surrender to this asshole either.

I lifted my chin. My knees didn't bend.

I was more prepared than when I'd confronted the Demigod of War, so I didn't even shudder, though inwardly, I was shaking a little.

A surprised, displeased expression flitted by the sea demigod's handsome, marble-like face.

Axel chuckled and smirked at his cousin, as if he realized what was going on and it made him giddy that I didn't cave to his cousin's bullying any more than I had his.

The others—the priest, the Dominion officers, and the initiates—didn't seem to have a clue that one of the demigods and I were engaged in a battle of wills before the trial had even begun.

As the sea demigod pushed harder and I pushed back to nullify his exertion, the priest opened the ceremony with a statement and introduced himself as Saint Theodore. Then he prayed to the twelve Olympian gods in his deep, musical voice, and finally moved on to praise the four demigods.

The Demigod of Sky—Zak, Demigod of Sea—Paxton, Demigod of Death—Héctor, and Demigod of War—Axel.

The Demigod of Death was the only one absent. He was the darkest, most mysterious super-being, since he held the door to death.

I was glad he wasn't around.

If he were here today, surely it would be to collect me and shove me to the other side of the veil, even though I wasn't ready. That was his specialty, wasn't it?

Zak flicked his gaze between his cousins and me for a brief second before closing his eyes, as if to meditate. He might be taking a nap, for all I knew.

Axel arched an eyebrow at me. If I read it right, he was asking me what I thought of his cousins.

Average assholes, I hissed in my mind.

Axel roared with laughter. All heads turned to him, but no one dared to ask what was so funny. If any of us had disturbed the beginning of a sacred ritual like that, we'd be dragged out to be executed.

Had he really read my thoughts?

Everyone knew that the sky demigod had the power of thunder and lightning, the sea demigod could cause tsunamis and flood cities, the death demigod collected souls, and the war demigod had all sorts of battle powers, including summoning storms in the battlefield.

No one had ever said they could read minds.

But then I'd tasted Axel's compulsion.

I'd better put on an extra mental shield when they were around.

Theodore paused in his speech. I wondered if he'd been reading the same script over and over about the gods' glory shining upon us and that we were so lucky to be chosen to receive the Blood Runes, which had created the elite gods' army and culled the unworthy for generations.

"Get a hold of yourself, Axel," Paxton hissed in a hushed voice from his throne.

"Or what?" Axel asked lazily, and then they were glaring at each other.

I wondered if the demigods picked fights with each other a lot.

Paxton had lost interest in making me kneel, but I still refrained from wiping the beads of sweat off my nose. My palms were also soaked in cold sweat after my efforts to resist his bullying power.

Axel stopped laughing after he spotted his priest's bewildered look.

"Don't mind me, good Theodore," the Demigod of War waved a hand. "Proceed and get them initiated according to the list of the names I gave you."

My heart rammed into my ribcage. Would he make me go first?

Theodore nodded dutifully. "As you wish, Demigod Axel." He surveyed us without interest and asked routinely, "Any questions?"

My eyes immediately brightened. This was my last chance.

I threw up two hands and shouted, "I have a question!" just in case he didn't see my hands.

Theodore looked surprised and not even a little bit pleased.

No one had ever asked him a question before? They couldn't just go along with whatever he said, right? What about free thinking?

And it was life and death in this ritual!

"Yes?" he asked in a clipped tone, and I forgave his baleful expression.

"I'm curious," I said. "How do you detect who has a god's DNA in them? Don't you want to perform a blood test first so you'll have a higher success rate getting the type of soldiers you want? Also so you won't drag a human into this mess and get him or her killed because he or she is just a human?"

"We don't drag humans into this sacred temple," Theodore said sternly. "A blood test, however, can't detect a god's genes in a candidate. We have our own method of locating prospective Dominion soldiers, which isn't your concern or for your ear. Now if you're done, be quiet and wait for your turn, *initiate*." His tone said I was done.

But I wasn't. Cameron had mentioned that they'd used a psychic ball to search for supernaturals. But the magic device had only found Jasper and Circe.

"Your psychic ball didn't see me," I said. "I'm not even on the chart of Dominion prospects. Demigod Axel brought me here by mistake. I think we should probably correct that before the ritual starts. There's no need to get messy."

The entire hall hushed to a complete silence. No one, to my knowledge, had ever accused a demigod of making a mistake, but this was my only chance to get the hell out of here.

It was now or never.

It wasn't simply the terror of death that made me fight either. Every fiber in me rebelled against the idea of having any outside force, like that ritual dagger, touch me or test me, as if I had a built-in failsafe and it screamed for me to run and never return.

Reflecting on it, I wondered if Vi might have known something about me. Maybe that was why she'd drilled it into my head to stay far away from any demon's or demigod's path at all costs.

I'd holed up in Crack until today, until both a demon and a demigod had shown up, and then shit just blew up.

I heard nasty growls. They were probably from Axel.

I avoided looking at him but gazed at the sky demigod hopefully. Among the three of them, he seemed the most sensible. He'd opened his eyes and learned forward on his throne to listen to me.

"I'm one hundred percent human," I hurried on. "I don't have an ounce of divine blood in me, not even remotely. Please dismiss me. If you want, you can send me to the Other Academy. I won't tell a soul about any of this. I swear. And as you can see, I haven't seen anything yet."

"Why did you bring a human into this, Axel?" Paxton turned his violet gaze on the war demigod with great displeasure. "You know the Half-Blood Academy isn't for humans. You've gone too far this time."

Zak swept his gaze from me to Axel, lightning flashing inside his blue eyes.

"Care to explain?" the sky demigod asked.

Axel rolled his eyes. "That little minx is devious. She's been hiding what she is from us for twenty years. I intend to find out who she really is. Only the Ritual of the Blood Runes will reveal her deepest secrets to us."

"I have no secrets," I shouted. "I am what you see. I'm a plain human and a nobody. Revered other demigods, I must appeal to you. Demigod Axel has a personal grudge against me because I refused to kneel in front of him. He brought me here to punish me severely. He wants to humiliate me before murdering me."

"That's a serious accusation against a demigod, initiate!" Theodore cut in, his silver eyes burning with fury. "No mortal has ever made such a claim. You'll be lucky to be struck to death by lightning when the judgment is over!"

He looked like he was about to throw a bolt of lightning at me or thrust the flaming dagger into my chest. I retreated half a step, darting my gaze around to see if I could find a weapon to fend for myself if a fight broke out.

"Silence, Theodore," Zak said. "Do not speak out of turn again."

The priest bowed in apology.

Silence stretched on in the hall.

I noticed that the three demigods shot glares at each other in odd ways. A thought hit me: damn, they were communicating telepathically.

Then both the sea and sky demigods sniffed the air.

Were they sniffing at me, as Axel had done earlier?

Panic spread through me when they traded another sinister, intrigued look.

All three pairs of demigod eyes trained on me, and I nearly shivered under the focus of their intense stares.

"We've voted," Zak announced. "All prospects will be initiated today. There'll be no exception. The weak will be weeded out, and the strong descendants of the gods will have their dormant powers activated and accentuated through the sacred Ritual of the Blood Runes."

There was nothing sacred about sacrificing an innocent life. But if I shouted my objections again, the demigod of lightning might just strike me down right now.

I had to take my chances with the ritual then.

A dark, yet hopeful thought wheeled through my head. I'd resisted two demigods' compulsion. I might just survive this fucking ritual.

I dropped my defeated gaze to the ground and waited for my name to be called. Asshole Axel had likely decided to let me die first.

When Demetra was called, I pressed my cold, sweat-soaked palms against the robe. I was relieved for a brief second, then I felt sorry for her, even though she was a bitch.

What if she didn't have a god's blood in her veins as she'd claimed? She could die!

Axel shifted his mischievous gaze back to me and smirked, and it dawned on me that I was the last on the list.

The fucker brought me here to play a sick game with me. He wanted me to watch a few agonizing deaths before I walked to my own.

I sent him a hateful stare before I let my burning gaze follow Demetra.

The blonde shot me an angry glare, as if I'd stolen her thunder or something, before she glided toward the operating table with a graceful gait, enjoying every minute of having the attention of the entire hall.

As she faced the demigods, she didn't show the slightest trait of a mean girl. She could appear to be the sweetest thing when she was dealing with someone above her rank.

Even the demigods' eyes slipped toward her, except for Axel's.

He still watched me closely, as if he wanted to record my every dreadful reaction.

Demetra flipped her hair like a siren queen before stepping onto the stool placed before the table. She perched on the edge of the table, facing the demigods with her ankles across each other perfectly, like a lady of great manners.

Theodore told her to open the top of her robe and lower it to just above her breasts, but Demetra pulled it all the way down to her waist, obviously wanting to give the demigods an eyeful.

The other demigods did give her exposed body a passing glance, but Axel kept his eyes glued on me.

Theodore frowned at the bountiful flesh in front of him—he was indeed a saint, even if he was a mean one—but in his eagerness to get to work, he didn't correct his first test object.

The dagger of fire in his hand, he approached her swiftly. From my angle I couldn't see exactly what he was doing, but from how the dagger danced, I speculated Theodore was carving the runes onto the skin beneath her left shoulder.

Either Theodore was skillful (he had to be adept, right, since he'd done this probably thousands of times?), or the tip of the blade barely touched her skin because Demetra only yelped a few times.

Theodore moved the blade away from her.

All three demigods were staring at her chest, and Zak nodded.

"Demetra is a descendant to Demeter, Goddess of Harvest and Fertility," Theodore announced. "She's one eighth goddess and also has a hint of siren heritage."

Demetra raised her chin high. At an eighth goddess, she was what she'd said she was, even if she'd exaggerated the percentage of her godly blood.

Even so, the hall gasped. She was indeed close to a demigoddess.

Theodore looked down at her and nodded. "Congratulations, Demetra. You've passed the first trial. You may return to your rank."

What? This was only the first trial?

Now I felt sorry for everyone.

Demetra glided back to our row as if she'd just been crowned. She shot me a haughty look. What had I done to her this time?

Then Jack was called and went through the same ritual. He proved to be a distant descendant of Zeus, but there was no shame of that. Most soldiers were a distant descendant, and Zeus was the current King of the Gods.

Then another clique boy was called. When the first rune hit his chest, he screamed and screamed, and then he dropped dead.

My blood went cold in my veins.

Two Dominion soldiers moved forward swiftly and removed the burned corpse.

Two other outsider initiates didn't make it either. They screamed and died.

Then it was Nat's turn. Yelena went all pale when his name was called. I grabbed her hand to support her, and she squeezed my hand back, hers shaking.

Nat made it. He was a distant descendant of Hephaestus, the God of Metal.

Then it was Yelena's turn, and I prayed for her to live. She and Nat were the only ones who were friendly to me.

Yelena turned out to be a not too distant descendant of Poseidon. Yet the Demigod of the Sea wasn't looking at the initiate who belonged to his house. He was looking at me.

Then my name was called.

I shot Axel a venomous look, and his dark eyebrow quirked, playing innocent. I could almost hear his silent question, "What was that for, darling?"

I was nowhere near as graceful as Demetra when I stepped onto the stool. Somehow my foot missed it, and I stumbled. But my hands caught the edge of the operating table.

A few snickers sounded from the clique.

Out of the twelve other initiates, five had perished, including a few members of their circle, and they didn't even care?

No one seemed to give a fuck except me. I mourned and was angered at the meaningless waste.

Theodore moved toward me with the flaming dagger in his hand.

"You sure you really want to do this?" I whispered, pleading, hoping a slice of compassion would rise in him.

Theodore only glared as if he'd had enough of me.

"A deal is a deal, Marigold," Axel said from his throne.

It was utterly pointless to argue with an asshole, especially a very powerful one.

I heard the sea demigod murmured something to Axel. "This girl tires me like no other. For centuries—since we started this ritual—we haven't met anyone as annoying and disrespectful and mouthy as her. If it were up to me, I'd just get rid of her right here, right now. I don't see why you're so obsessed. But then you're almost as young as she is."

Ignoring Paxton's snide comments, Axel rose from his throne and strode toward me, power trailing behind him like silver shadows.

Unlike the other two demigods, he wore a dress shirt, denim pants, and a fashionable trench coat. I tore my gaze from roving over his cut chest to his powerful legs. That might be the last sexy sight I'd see.

For a second there, he seemed just like any other hot guy a normal girl would love to go out with. For a second, I completely forgot where I was and that he was the Demigod of War.

Damn you, girl! I scolded myself. *Death is waving at you, and you still ogle the demigod who brought you this grief?*

I straightened my back, determined to go out with dignity.

It didn't matter, though. I shouldn't even bother with my posture. There was no dignity in death.

"Go on then," I said to the priest. "Cut me if you must. Carve whatever runes you like on my skin. But I'd rather die standing than—"

CHAPTER 7

Before I finished my sentence, Theodore's dagger shot a stream of flame toward me, hotter than imaginary dragon fire.

"What the fuck are you doing?" I cried.

That wasn't what happened with any of the other initiates. Theodore must be so pissed he intended to burn me instead of carving the runes on my skin with care and skill.

Instinctively, I threw up my hands to fend off the fire, even though it was a pathetic, futile gesture.

The flame socked into my chest so hard I flew backward and rammed into the operating table. The table flew up and smashed into a splendid chandelier high up on the ceiling. A sharp crash of steel hitting glass sounded throughout the temple.

Crystals and diamonds rained down, and the initiates beneath them ducked.

The table flew across the room at an odd angle. It must have hit a few soldiers, judging from the curses and groans of pain.

"What the fuck?" Axel roared in rage, zooming toward me.

"I didn't do that!" Theodore shouted. "I haven't touched the girl. The dagger acted on its own. This has never happened in millennia. Something doesn't add up. It must be the girl. No one has ever dared to ask questions during the ritual. She talked too much."

Fury burst through me that they were trying to make the whole thing my fault when I was the one who'd gotten hit.

Nervous whispers churned through the hall as everyone seemed to have something to say.

"The Ritual of the Blood Runes is to weed out the weak, the unworthy, and the unfit. It leaves only the strong to defend humanity," Demetra said, probably to her clique or anyone who was willing to listen. "That's the unbreakable tradition of the first ceremony in the Half-Blood Academy. I knew that rogue would be incinerated."

"Shut up," Yelena hissed. "If you still have a thread of humanity left."

"How dare you rebuke me, you stupid cow?" Demetra asked.

"Don't you call her a cow, you viper!" Nat said. "And you aren't a quarter as you falsely claimed. You're but one-eighth. That's a huge difference."

"Yet I'm still far more advanced than any of you," Demetra retorted.

I no longer heard their quarrel or was even concerned about it since I had to put out the fire on my person.

I refused to go down without a fight.

All the demigods surrounded me in an instant.

I looked down at my chest, expecting a burning hole, but it wasn't like that. The flame had turned out to be runes writing themselves on my skin in shifting colors—crimson first, then black, purple, blue, golden…

The runes didn't limit themselves to the space between my left shoulder blade and the top of my left breast, where they were supposed to go. They crawled all over my torso. Crimson, golden, and black runes formed shapes and lines and disappeared, then moved in shapes again on my shoulders, arms, and breasts, like a whole freak show.

Axel looked so awed. I stared at him and then back to the crawling runes in horror.

He pulled my robe down from my shoulders without my permission, and I was too freaked out and too busy watching the runes to punch him in the jaw.

"All twelve of the runes have imprinted on you," Axel declared. "That's incredible."

"It's impossible. She can't be a descendant of all twelve major gods! No one can," Theodore said, his silver eyes widening, but he was elbowed out of the way.

The demigods were in charge now.

The dagger in Theodore's hand dulled, and the flame vanquished.

"My blade!" Theodore called. "Both the flame and runes are gone."

"She absorbed all of them," Zak said, lightning twirling in his royal blue eyes as he studied me like he'd just seen me, truly seen me. "She's taken all of them as if they were her birthright."

The runes still twirled all over my body as if trying to decide where they should settle down.

"Just make up your mind already," I groaned.

Axel tore his gaze from the runes and smiled at me. "You live, Marigold," he said. "Just as I believed that you'd prevail."

He gave the impression he wanted to pull me into an embrace to congratulate me, but I was still so mad at him that I shoved him away, then I put a hand up to prevent him, or any of them, from getting closer to me.

I had no idea what these runes were going to do to me and was terrified they'd change who I was. I was comfortable with the old Marigold. But a primal part of me already knew that the blood runes had triggered something dark and dangerous, something that had been buried deep inside me.

"Remove the runes, please," I said harshly. "I don't want them."

That was when the burn started.

Embers of fire sparked off my skin. Then the runes turned to leaping flames. In an instant, I became a human torch from inside out.

Agony tore through me, and I howled.

"What's going on?" Axel shouted, face paling. "Ice, Paxton!"

The Demigod of Sea conjured icy currents and poured them onto me.

The fire burning inside me hissed and sizzled, turning hotter.

"Stop!" I screamed.

The fucker was making it worse.

"It's not working," Paxton said in dismay. "She's burning from the inside."

No duh, asshole!

"Help her!" Axel screamed. "How could this happen? Theodore, you're the fucking priest. You know all the runes. If you don't fix her, I'll skin you alive!"

"I don't know how," Theodore yelled back. "It wasn't supposed to happen like this. As I said, this has never happened before."

Axel's icy wind slammed into me as I rolled and writhed on the ground, tearing my robe off in agony and shrieking as the fire scorched me like hellfire from the inferno—not that I'd ever visited Hell.

This was Hell.

"Get out!" Zak shouted at the Dominion soldiers and the other initiates, and the hall emptied in seconds except for the demigods and their priest.

For a nanosecond, I was grateful to him for preserving my last scrap of dignity.

"Hang in there, Marigold," Axel shouted, crouching beside me, devastation written all over his face. Like he cared! He'd brought me to this. "We'll figure out a way to stop the burn."

"She must have hidden power that we don't know about," Theodore diagnosed, as he and the demigods all squatted around me, peering down at me. "The runes are sentient, but they haven't been this active for centuries. It must be her power calling the runes' power. When they sensed the power in her, they jumped to her without me etching a basic rune on her.

"She insisted she was human, but you said she was anything but human, right, Demigod Axel? You must have sensed the power in her, too. I think you're right. The runes have triggered or activated her veiled powers, as they were designed to do. I believe that she contains more than one god's power, and the powers in her are fighting for dominance."

"This makes no sense. How can all twelve runes choose her?" Zak said. "We're the demigods, the most powerful beings on Earth. Even we don't have all the powers. Even we have less than three dominant powers. I need to call my father."

"By the time you get a hold of Zeus, Marigold might be dead," Axel grated. "I'm calling my father now. At least he's on Earth."

"But Ares is in the battle zone with Lucifer," Paxton said. "Aren't they negotiating another treaty now?"

While the bastards kept debating, fire boiled every inch of my skin. At this point, I wanted only death. I couldn't bear another second of this torment.

"Behead me," I shouted as I clawed my skin to expel the fire or the poisonous runes. "End this torture now, Axel, and I'll forgive you for this hell you brought me to."

"I can't," he said. His hand touched my face. "I can't let you die. Please, give me a bit more time and let us figure out how to save you."

"There's no saving me," I screamed. "Give me a quick death!"

I lunged for the ritual dagger, still in Theodore's hand, determined to slice my own throat and end this. But that fucker ducked away swiftly, and the force of fire dropped me on the ground again.

When a new wave of agony hit me, I lost my shit.

I cursed the demigods between my hoarse screams. "Fuck you! Who gave you the fucking right to decide who's worthy? I had a good life, fuckers! At least I was free and had friends... and you had to rip that life from me and send me to this inferno."

From the reflection in Axel's grief-stricken eyes, I could see my eyes glowing red.

I saw red.

I wanted to kill him. I wanted to kill them all.

"I'm a human. I can't contain the runes, assholes," I shouted in rage. "A human life means nothing to you. My life means nothing to you."

"If you were a human, you'd have been burned to ashes by now," Theodore argued.

What nerve he had! How could I pass this burn to him?

"Shush, Marigold," Axel tried to calm me. "Your life means everything to me. I've opened a link to my father and called for his immediate assistance. He's coming, and we'll figure it out. We'll save you."

"Yeah, you just keep saying that, you lying son of a bitch," I shouted and sobbed and screamed. And when I cursed, I felt a bit better. "All you want is to win the war against the demons, so you have to drag everyone you think can fight into your Dominion ranks. Five initiates died today. Actually six, since I'll soon join them. I'm only twenty. I haven't even really lived. And I'm still a fucking virgin! Damn you! Damn you all. After my death, I'll come to haunt you as a ghost, a poltergeist, actually. I'll be worse than the devils you fight. I'll be your everyday's fucking nightmare. Especially Axel! I'll haunt you! You won't have a second of fucking peace…"

"Blasphemy!" Theodore said. "I've never heard anyone curse so much. We should just give her what she wants and end her."

"Shut up, Theodore," Axel said. "Touch her, and I'll end you."

Then I was lifted off the ground while I thrashed violently.

The next moment, I was in Axel's arms. "I won't let you die," he said. "Let me take the burn for you. If we die, we die together."

The merciless fire leapt from me to him, eager to find a new host, even though it still roasted me.

Agony twisted the handsome face of the Demigod of War, but he suppressed a scream and only held me tighter.

Shock slammed into me, despite the awful fire still inside me.

I'd never expected anyone, least of all a demigod, to do this for me, even though he'd brought me to this stage in the first place.

A demigod would never sacrifice himself for a mortal. They were notorious for being the most selfish, self-serving bastards on the planet.

But Axel was ready to die for me—or with me.

"No." I struggled in his arms. "Just kill me."

"Perhaps with our combined powers, the fire will distribute among us instead of burning her alone," Zak said, and he embraced me, too.

Then I felt the Demigod of Sea join us.

"What are you doing?" Theodore shouted. "You're the immortal demigods, but you can still be killed. You can't waste your lives for a girl you barely know."

The demigods let the fire burn them as well as they kept pouring their power into me to shield me.

A stream of cool air coursed through my veins.

Then, all of a sudden, the fire vanished and the burning ceased.

I slumped in Axel's arms, still murmuring about haunting them as a vengeful ghost.

"Stop babbling, Cookie," Axel whispered. "You'll live. You survived."

Who was Cookie? Were there cookies around?

"Cookies?" I choked. "I want one. And where am I?"

"In my arms," he said, and then he kissed me.

I didn't know what had gotten into me, but I wasn't in my strongest state or my right mind. I didn't resist him, even though I still hated him.

The Demigod of War tasted me as if I was the most delicious thing he'd ever tried.

I liked his pure male scent, like the wind and the burning stars—even though I'd just gotten burned.

I stretched against his hard torso, threaded my fingers into his rich brown hair, and grabbed hold to anchor myself.

Our kiss deepened, and instantly, liquid fire twirled between my thighs.

I vaguely remembered that I wasn't wearing panties, but I didn't remember why I hadn't put them on in the first place.

A new kind of desire seared me, unlike anything I'd experienced.

I arched my back and pressed tighter against my enemy, knowing that I wanted him more than the world.

A rough groan rumbled from his chest.

Axel's lust slammed into me like hard steel and nectar at once. He was the Demigod of War, so even his desire was warlike, yet it turned me on like no one ever had.

I'd become a Marigold I barely recognized.

Axel pulled away from me, and I glared at him for depriving me of the carnal pleasure of his mouth and body.

He chuckled darkly, prying my fingers off the locks of his lush hair.

"We have to stop now, Cookie," he said. "Or I won't be able to stop. I'll do wicked things to you, dirty and wicked things."

I parted my lips and blinked at him incredulously.

Then slowly, common sense returned to me.

The vast Hall of Olympia was eerily quiet, my throat raw and hoarse, and I recalled that I'd almost burned to a pile of ashes.

Two other demigods and the priest stared at me as if I'd grown a demon horn.

I swept a shaking hand over my head to make sure I hadn't.

Relieved that I might still be me, I turned my glare to Axel. "How dare you kiss me!"

My voice was harsh, even though my lips begged for another kiss.

I didn't want to admit it, but his taste was as addictive as drugs.

There was magic in the demigod's kiss.

He smirked at me. "You kissed me back."

"I didn't," I said. "And even if I did, I wasn't exactly myself."

"Are you yourself now?" he asked gently. "Let's get you settled down, Cookie. You need rest. You've had quite a shock today."

His thumb wiped away my lingering tears. He slid his thumb between his lips, licking off my tears with a heated gaze, as if he wanted to discern if there was fire or magic in it.

Suddenly, another strong hand pulled me away from Axel, and I found myself in Zak's arms.

The Demigod of War growled.

"I shielded her. I saved her, too," Zak said. "So it's my turn."

His turn for what?

And he slanted his mouth over mine and kissed me as well.

What? Now I was their prize, a reward because I'd lived?

But the Demigod of Sky smelled really good, like sandalwood and sunlight and powerful sex. I should slap him to show that I still had some dignity and sense, but I wanted a bit more of him, too.

His sky power enveloped me, and a trace of his lightning fell on my skin, sparkling like tiny fireworks. It didn't hurt, but sent a shiver of pleasure all the way from my breasts down to my toes.

My exhaustion faded, and my lust piqued like a beast at my new object of interest.

I grabbed his face to pull him closer.

I wanted him as much as I desired Axel.

My hunger for the demigods was so primal it stunned me.

The ritual had messed me up big time. I felt different now that the runes had sunk into my body. I couldn't tell if I liked this version of me or not, but I felt powerful and liberated.

Something soul-deep within me wanted to merge with the Demigod of Sky, to be one with him and his power, to mate with him and claim him. Driven by a savage need, I kissed him with bruising force.

Zak chuckled against my lips at my possessive display, and Axel growled a warning.

The Demigod of Sea remained quiet, but his power refused to stay put; it crushed into me like waves, soaking me with his disapproval and dark need at the same time.

"That's enough, Zak," Axel said. "She's mine. I saw her first."

He shoved himself like a wedge between us and glared at the sky demigod.

Zak's sky-blue gaze stayed on me, bright and awed and full of desire.

Axel didn't miss a beat and wrapped around me, as if he was afraid that someone else would take me away.

"Be gentle with her!" he barked. "She's still in shock."

"She aroused all three of us," Paxton said in a tone curling with dark anger. "No woman has ever done that."

He said it like it was my fault. What was his problem?

"Haven't you seen what the runes did to her?" Axel hissed. "It set her on fire from within! She can't be responsible for her actions right now. I won't let anyone take advantage of her while she's vulnerable."

"What about you?" Zak asked. "Who's to protect her from you then?"

"I'd never hurt her," Axel said.

Zak folded his muscled arms before his broad chest and snorted.

"She doesn't seem fragile to me, even after what happened to her," Paxton said. "She's more like a she-shark that's ready to bite."

"I'm still here, in case you jerks haven't noticed," I hissed. "And is there even a she-shark? How can you know the sex of a shark? Do you flip it around and take a peek? I don't think the shark will be so pleased at your poke."

Axel laughed. "That's my girl, as fun as ever."

Paxton gave me a look. "I'm the Demigod of Sea. I know my shit."

Zak chortled, running a hand over his cropped hair. "Marigold's bite was actually delicious. I haven't tasted the like for ages."

"We're done here," Axel growled. "Marigold has had enough. She won't put up with any more frivolousness."

He put his trench coat over me and scooped me up, and I clung to him like a vine while gazing up at him expectantly, hoping he would grace me with another hot kiss.

I hadn't savored him enough when he kissed me so briefly.

The old Marigold was thinking how crazy it was for me to have kissed two demigods. I barely knew them. But after the runes had jumped my bones and turned to nasty flames, maybe I deserved a little break with a big distraction?

"She isn't yours alone, Axel," said the Demigod of Sea. "Since you both kissed her, I demand the same courtesy. I did save her, too."

I turned to him, licking my swollen lips—the result of being kissed by two demigods. Paxton was a knockout. His flowing silver hair framed a perfect, masculine face that seemed carved out of the purest, hardest ice. His body every defined muscle exuding power—was every woman's wet dream.

I was slick between my thighs, and I lusted after him as well.

However, I was also pissed.

He hadn't been remotely friendly toward me, even though he'd helped put out the fire inside me along with other demigods.

He demanded to kiss me. He hadn't even bothered to ask if I wanted it or not. He thought he could stake his claim as he saw fit. I bet he was the entitled jackass type who had always taken what he wanted. I bet he'd treated women as disposable pleasures, barely appreciating them, like we were trash.

Some women might overlook his flaws and swarm to him because he was gorgeous and powerful, but I'd never date an asshole. I wouldn't give him an inch.

I met his violet, bedroom eyes. The cockiness and dark hunger in them made my heart flutter for a second.

But I knew that if you played with a villain, you'd get burned.

I'd been cooked by the flame, literally, and the last thing I wanted was to be a stupid moth.

"I'm not a trophy, dude," I told the Demigod of Sea. "I'm not kissing anyone anymore."

"But you let them kiss you, didn't you?" Paxton said, narrowing his eyes.

"I wasn't myself," I said. "But I'm starting to feel better. I don't want to get involved with any of you." I waved a hand in exasperation and tried to extricate myself from Axel's arms. "Why am I even explaining this to you? Who I kiss is no one's business but my own."

"You do realize that by turning me down you're making an enemy out of me?" the sea demigod asked. Menace rolled off him like a physical thing, rubbing and bruising my skin.

Fury shot through me.

I twisted in Axel's arms, struggling to land on the ground and stand on my own feet.

"Deal with it, jerk," I hissed. "Rejection is a part of life. And I don't take threats kindly."

He stalked toward me, violence in his eyes, but Zak stepped between us.

Axel moved me behind him, ready to go to war with Paxton.

The Demigod of Sea halted, slanting us a measured look, and an impish smile stretched his sensual lips.

No matter how he pulled up his bad boy charm, it wouldn't touch me. I shored up the steel walls of my will, checking my defenses against his charisma and my newly raging libido.

"So that's how it's going to be now?" Paxton asked. "You two let a woman divide us? You know how it will end."

"Back off, Paxton," Axel said. "I won't say it again. Marigold has had enough today, so stop being a dick."

"Chill out, Paxton," Zak also said.

Paxton stepped back. "For now, I'll leave her alone."

"You all can address me directly," I said hotly. "I'm in the room."

If they thought they were above me, I was more than happy to shatter their illusions. No one was above anyone. That was basic courtesy.

"You absorbed my lightning power, Marigold," Zak said.

I had felt energized since he'd sent his lightning to caress me while we were kissing, almost as if it'd restored me after the draining power of the fire.

Had he kissed me to test me?

But his kiss and touch had been more than that. I'd felt his raw desire and hunger as intense as Axel's.

Theodore coughed from a few paces away.

"Pardon me, demigods," Theodore said. "If you're all done kissing or talking about kissing, we need to focus on finding out from whom the girl descends."

"Let's see what she's got," Paxton said almost viciously.

If I belonged to his house, he'd have jurisdiction over me, so I prayed that whatever power I had, it had nothing to do with Poseidon.

Axel picked me up again. Before I could lodge a protest, he'd carried me to his throne and put me down on it. Shock stilled my tongue. Even though no one was attending the demigods' court now to see it, it felt like Axel was sharing his power with me—or at least regarded me as his equal, which, as far as I knew, a demigod had never done before.

Or maybe it was just Axel's way of apologizing to me.

I blinked in confusion, bracing for the other demigods to object to me being on one of the thrones, but none of them seemed the least concerned.

Oh, Theodore looked a bit taken aback at where I was, but he didn't issue an opinion. He probably wouldn't want to draw fire from the Demigod of War.

"Cookie," Axel said, his tone cajoling.

I frowned at him for giving me the nickname Cookie, even if I liked cookies a bit too much. Who wouldn't? Especially macaroons, which were an absolutely sinful indulgence.

Zak arched an eyebrow at the name. Paxton snorted through his snooty nose as if to say he regarded me as anything but a sweet, delicious Cookie.

Axel smiled at me disarmingly, but I didn't buy it.

"We need to see the symbols on you to know which house you belong to," Axel said.

I didn't want any of them to see, but it was inevitable. They had to know my bloodline.

I shrugged off his trench coat. My robe was in tatters.

I gazed down at the space between my left shoulder blade and left breast, but I didn't spot any symbols.

"There's nothing," I said in shock.

"There's nothing on her skin," Theodore echoed his surprise.

"But we saw all twelve runes imprint when the flame burned her," Zak said. "Maybe the symbols settled somewhere else on her person."

On a place where the sun didn't shine? I nearly snickered.

Of course, they would demand to examine my body to search for a symbol, any symbol, and I couldn't fend off all of them if they were really determined. Besides, I wanted to know if there was any foreign mark on my body, too.

I pulled the scraps of the robe down to my waist, and all three demigods stared at my breasts point blank instead of looking for the symbol they were supposed to find.

They hadn't even glanced at other female initiates' breasts when they showed theirs—okay, except Demetra's perfect ones.

I glared at them. "Not like I have three tits, guys."

A hand moved toward my breast, and to my surprise, it belonged to Saint Theodore.

"Fuck off, Theodore," Axel snarled, shoving the saint away. "Who gave you permission to touch Marigold?"

Both Zak and Paxton growled at the priest threateningly as well.

Theodore stumbled back and raised his hands in a gesture of yielding.

"I don't share the same interest that you have in Marigold," he protested. "There isn't a burn mark on her skin. Not even a blister, despite how hard the flame ravaged her. I just want to touch her skin to make sure what I see is real."

"You're lucky we even let you look," Axel grated.

I quickly glanced down at my skin. It was golden, tanned, and as smooth as silk.

"Like the view, gentlemen?" I snickered as I noticed that their eyes still glued to my breasts. "Are you going to keep staring at my breasts or start helping me look for any hidden symbols?"

Axel chuckled. "My Cookie."

The demigods tore their eyes from my breasts and started examining the rest of my body with grumpy attitudes.

"This kitten doesn't know when to keep her mouth shut," Paxton said as he moved behind me to check my back. "We'll have to tame her first if we want to make her ours."

What? Tame me? Theirs?

Had he meant that they would share me and make me their plaything? That would happen when Hell froze.

"I'm not yours," I said.

"Not yet," Zak said positively.

"You're certainly welcome to try," I said. "Your fantasy will come true when the sun truly shines out of your asses."

Axel laughed like he didn't believe I was serious.

Would I want to be funny after I'd just been burned? The demigods could be really apathetic and self-centered, even the young Demigod of War. I bet those qualities were their gods' family traits.

If I were ever up to the job, I might just be the woman who could teach all of them a lesson.

Zak shook his head, but didn't say anything more.

Paxton, however, wasn't even slightly amused at my rude analogy. "Is that a challenge?" he asked in a flat tone that contained more than a little menace.

Zak and Axel shot him a warning look.

"I won't just bend you, *Princesa*," Paxton continued, ignoring Zak and Axel. "I'll break you. You might have my two cousins wrapped around your little fingers with your exotic looks, but neither of them will be able to stop me if you get on my bad side—I'll take you out, mortal. And you haven't met the heartless Demigod of Death. No man or woman can bewitch him. No one touches him and lives."

Princesa meant princess in Spanish. The Demigod of Sea was mocking me. I was as far from a princess as anyone could get. I was raised in the streets, in the hood. Paxton was simply reminding me that I was a street rat by calling me princess. I bet Axel had briefed his demigod cousins about where he'd rounded me up.

"Will you stop terrorizing Marigold?" Axel challenged back. "You know I'm on her side."

Paxton graced Axel with a glance. "Even Zak takes your side since the two of you share the same house, but Héctor will always be in my corner. And I want you two to remember we agreed not to fight over a woman."

"I might have lavender hair," I said in a snide tone as I shoved a fist into the air, "but my look is far from exotic. It's an everyday, regular girl's look. And secondly—"

Axel pulled my fist down. "Don't aggravate him while you're still in a delicate state, Cookie,"

"Don't put her and Paxton alone in a room," Zak declared. "And we'll avert a disaster."

Theodore frowned deeply as he wheeled around me, still trying to locate a symbol of a god's power on my skin or maybe wait for it to appear.

"She might not even be a mortal," the priest said. "No mortal could live through channeling divine fire. Even a demigod can't take it alone. The runes with the combined powers of the twelve major gods would leave an imprint on a god as well."

"Are you saying she's above us?" Paxton snarled. "Be careful with your words."

Theodore startled. "Of course not. That's blasphemy. As your priest, I'd never commit such a sin. However, Marigold is the first unknown to us. An utter mystery. What I'm saying is she could be an immortal, but to find out what she really is, we may have to wait for time to tell. Her powers will eventually manifest, and then we'll decide what to do with her."

I felt a chill down my spine. What were they going to do with me if they decided I wasn't what they were looking for?

"I don't think we're ever going to find a rune mark or any symbol of any god's house on me," I said, pulling Axel's trench coat tightly around me. "Which only means one thing."

"What is that, Cookie?" Axel asked in concern.

"Yeah, what is that, *Princesa*?" Paxton asked arrogantly as he returned to standing in front of me with his arms folded across his chest.

I smirked, feeling victorious for the first time since the Dominions had rounded up my team and me.

I'd defied their rules.

I'd confused all three demigods and their priest.

Axel had forced me to come here. Paxton and Zak had refused to listen to reason when I'd pleaded with them. They'd screwed me big, and I screwed them right back, giving them no answers and no satisfaction.

I wasn't sure if it was because I was so stubborn that I'd beat the demigods at their own game or because I was something else that granted me the power to cancel out the runes.

The important thing was: these assholes couldn't figure me out.

I hoped they never would.

"It means I don't come from the Olympian gods' bloodlines," I said giddily. "I don't belong to any of your houses since I'm not a descendant, unlike the surviving initiates and your Dominion soldiers. You have no right to hold me here. You must release me immediately!"

"Like hell we'll ever let you go," Zak said. The sudden possessiveness in his voice took me aback.

"But I don't belong in Half-Blood Academy," I shouted. "If you want me to stay, you can send me to the Other

Academy. I'll fit right in there." I wanted to be with Jasper and Circe, the only family I had. "As Saint Theodore said," I continued, lowering my voice a little at the demigods' dark looks, "I'm clearly not exactly a human. But since I'm not your kind either, I must be some other kind, something like a witch. I'll just pack my stuff and go to the Other Academy."

I didn't have any stuff. I'd be just packing myself.

I jumped up from Axel's throne, but Zak caught me.

He held my chin with his thumb and forefinger. "You'll stay with us. We'll train you in person to make your power manifest. We'll help you figure it out."

I stared at the demigods in dismay while Paxton offered me a villainous smile.

I had a terrible feeling they'd never leave me alone and they'd never let me go, no matter what.

CHAPTER 8

I was sharing a dormitory with seven other girls.

Fortunately, Demetra didn't share the room with us. If she had, I would never have slept with both eyes closed. But Demetra and her minions holed up in the dorm across the hallway from us.

The two girls whose bunk beds neared the door were second-year students. Four other first-years had been enrolled four months ago, so Yelena and I seemed to have a lot to catch up on and a big gap to shorten.

However, I didn't feel the pressure as much as my friend did. I was probably the only one in the Academy who had no ambition to be at the top of the class—or even to graduate—or to catch the demigods' eyes.

I didn't mind failing an exam. Actually, I aimed for failing.

I was born a hunter, not some Dominion drone who put up with all sorts of crap and took orders from every shitty jerk above my rank.

I definitely had issues with authority.

The demigods were welcome to kick me out at anytime or kiss my ass.

My bunkmates insisted on me showing them my mark. Finally, I caved. We weren't senior-year students, so we weren't granted a private bathroom. They'd catch me naked in the public bath chamber eventually.

"You don't have any symbol on your skin, Marigold," one of my bunkmates, Autumn, cried in alarm. "Everyone receives a power symbol on their skin to indicate which god's house they belong to. How come you didn't get one, even though you survived the ritual?"

"The demigods wondered the same thing," I said drily. "For all I care what they think. Even Theodore couldn't figure out shit."

"Looks to me like you don't belong to any god's house," said Misty, a first-year girl who was a bit meaner than the others. "You're lucky they haven't kicked you out."

"I hope my luck runs out soon," I said.

Yelena held both of my hands in sympathy. I actually didn't like people holding my hands like that, as if I needed loads of tissues to wipe my teary face, but she was trying to offer moral support.

One did not dismiss kindness.

"An icon will eventually show up on Marigold's shoulder," Yelena said, defending me. "She's just one of those late bloomers."

"I heard the divine flame jumped on you." Samantha, a second-year, sent me a pitiful look. "But no one knew what happened afterwards since the demigods kicked everyone out after you screamed bloody hell. What really happened?"

The girls all pricked up their ears.

I wasn't going to confide in them. Not a damn thing. I definitely wasn't going to tell them that two demigods kissed me and one threatened me.

They weren't my people.

"Nothing really happened. The fire went out, and the priest sent me back here." I yawned. "I'm going to call it a night. I have an early class tomorrow."

The last thing I wanted was for the whole Academy to know the ritual had probably turned me into a freak. Thankfully, my bunkmates, who had short attention span, soon lost interest in me.

Yeah, I'd lived. Yet I had a bad feeling that surviving the flame was just the beginning of a series of bad things.

First off, unlike everyone else, I didn't get a power upgrade after the Ritual of the Blood Runes. I neither rose nor fell. I just got burned.

I was also the only one who hadn't had an orientation. And from what I'd learned so far, Yelena and I were the first years most likely to be treated as a snack between the teeth of the sharks in this predator-infested pool.

Yelena squeezed my hands one last time before she returned to her own bunk. "The most important thing is that you passed the trial. No one thought you would survive the flame, but you did."

She meant that the clique talked shit about me afterwards. Yelena had briefed me on how Demetra had complained to no end about me holding up the demigods with my stinky stunt during the sacred ritual.

Well, I'd love to give her the honor of having endured burning to catch the demigods'—or any god's—attention. Demetra had been even more bitter that Axel had personally carried me to the bunk while I slept in his arms.

I didn't remember that the Demigod of War had delivered me here. I'd passed out at some point after the demigods' bickering in the Hall of Olympia.

"According to Demetra, they should have just put you in a wheelchair and had a junior escort you to the bunk room,"

Yelena had said with laughter. "Everyone can see that the Demigod of War has a soft spot for you."

And I'd made an enemy out of the Demigod of Sea.

But who gave a shit about the swimming boy?

I lifted my fingers to count how many enemies I already had in this new school—Paxton, Demetra, their goons, and who else?

I hoped all the bullies wouldn't think to combine forces, but I had a foreboding feeling that they might. An army of bullies would come for my blood, led by a demigod.

According to the intel gathered by Nat, who'd turned out to be a resourceful, good-looking gay man, Demetra had influence at the Academy because of her filthy rich family.

Even though the demigods headed all the Half-Blood Academies, they didn't exactly run the schools. They had no patience for or interest in any administrative duties.

No, pretty much they just popped in and out of the Half-Blood academies all over the globe and focused most of their time on the war against the demons.

Their favorite hangouts weren't in the schools but in the war zones.

It was rare that all four demigods were in one place at the same time, so everyone here in the North American academy was thrilled, especially all the girls.

In less than twenty-four hours, I'd heard more gossip about the demigods than I'd heard in my past twenty years.

As my thoughts drifted away, the girls were still eagerly arguing over which demigod was the hottest and betting on who would be lucky enough to be chosen as the demigods' next lovers.

Four out of the six girls voted for the death demigod as the sexiest and most mysterious hunk, but he was utterly unattainable, which made him even more sought-after.

Suddenly, their talk piqued my interest.

Paxton had said he and Héctor would unite against me. I needed to know more about my enemies, especially the one I hadn't met.

"Why is he unattainable?" I asked.

"You don't know anything about the demigods' world, do you?" Neha, another first-year, asked. "Which rock have you been living under?"

"My own rock?" I said.

"Good thing you've finally crawled out from under it," Neha snorted.

"I was forced out," I said. "I was quite comfortable living under the rocks, you know."

"You're hopeless," she said. "Why was I even talking to you?"

"You're still talking," I said.

"Yeah, just a warning: watch where you're going," she said.

It wasn't news that the new students were often treated as punching bags.

Though most of the girls in this dormitory were also first-years, they were ahead of Yelena and me. They held to the military tradition that they had every right to treat the newbies however they saw fit. I'd already seen a new initiate get kicked in the head when an upperclassman was in a foul mood.

I vowed secretly that if anyone came at either Yelena or me, they'd learn that harassing us was more trouble than it was worth.

"No one can stand Demigod Héctor's touch," Yelena said, coming to my rescue again. It was evident that I was the only one who lived under a rock coated with so much ignorant moss. "Whomever he touches dies instantly."

"I hope I can have the same ability," I said longingly, thinking of all the enemies I had. "I want to be in his house."

"Héctor is very lonely," Neha said, as if she personally knew him. "I feel so bad for him. All his sexiness gets wasted like that."

So the Demigod of Death ranked number one in the Academy libidos because of his lethal touch combined with his natural damn sex appeal and, of course, perfect male torso.

I wasn't surprised that the girls voted Axel as number two, but I was astonished to find out he was actually a fourth year student in Half-Blood Academy.

He was a demigod, so he didn't obey any of the rules. He skipped most of his classes and only popped in every now and then to poke fun of the professors or cause some trouble for everyone. Otherwise he was in the war zone with his father or, according to gossip, making time with his pick of the women on campus.

Goddamnit, the Demigod of War wasn't much older than me, and I'd thought he was ancient, like the other demigods.

Next time he pissed me off, I'd tell him he ranked as the least hot demigod in the Academy because of his baby face. I bet it'd leave a big bruise on his oversized ego.

The number three crown went to Paxton, who was mostly feared.

"Getting on his bad side is like having a death mark branded on your forehead," Jessica, another first-year, whispered with a shiver. "But he's so hot. I could just watch his rippling muscles move all day long. Last time when he strode toward me with those powerful legs, I almost passed out at the sight of him."

Poor Zak was listed as number four, probably because he kept the most distance from the recruits and was way too serious. He never smiled.

According to my bunkmates, he was eons old and the most powerful of the demigods. He was one of the first-born demigods and had just returned to Earth a century ago when the gods' war with the demons summoned him here.

With a life that long, who wouldn't grow apathetic? I kind of felt sorry for him. Immortality could be a curse.

Paxton had been born when the war between Lucifer and Ares had just started. He was basically the product of war. No wonder he was the nastiest of them all. There was probably nothing but violence surrounding him when he grew up, which definitely would shape his worldview and personality.

So, *this* was academy life?

During daytime, we attended classes and beat the shit out of each other; at night, the girls gossiped about hot boys—practically drooling over them, especially the demigods—without any filter.

I wondered what the male students talked about in their bunks.

When the girls' discussion circled back to the lonely hotness of the death demigod, I snuggled under the blanket and rolled my eyes.

I wondered how Jasper and Circe were doing and if they'd settled down well.

I didn't know what tomorrow would bring me, but after only a day in the Academy, I wasn't looking forward to it.

CHAPTER 9

I wasn't sure if this was a dream or what—it felt more real than anything in my waking life. But I had no idea how I'd gotten here.

I was in an opulent apartment in a skyscraper. Through floor-to-ceiling windows, I looked down on a lush park of green and pink. Opposite that window was another overlooking a bustling city under my feet.

Parts of the city had burned. Clusters of fire still smoldered in some buildings, their smoke trails whirling into the windy sky.

It must be the war zone, but I hadn't spotted Dominion soldiers fighting horned demons down there. Maybe it was too far away for me to see the battle unfolding, or maybe both sides were in a recess.

Everyone needed a lunch break, right? Except the scavengers who dashed out of broken buildings and stores and scattered through the streets, collecting what they could find.

I trained my sights on the intact part of the city where people went on with their lives—crowds in the prosperous commercial districts and streets—strolling, shopping, skateboarding, or burying their faces into their phones, probably texting or something.

I'd never in my life used a phone—nobody in Crack did—but I'd heard that social media was still a thing in the parts of the world controlled by the demigods.

The Olympian gods wanted civilization to continue on, while, according to rumor, Lucifer didn't care much about it, particularly not social media. He wasn't exactly a popular guy in any non-demon city. He wasn't even popular in Crack, but neither were the demigods.

I swept my gaze around the apartment, and my breath caught when I spotted the most stunning view through glass doors that led to a spacious balcony. A pair of massive, black wings spread to their glorious, full length, soaking in twilight.

As they slowly, lazily folded and then vanished, I found myself staring at the bare torso of a giant male who perched on a chair custom-made to accommodate his wings. Taut muscles rippled across his bulging arms and beautiful back as he ran a hand over the thick mane of his dark hair.

I hadn't met anyone more mesmerizing than this specimen, even though I hadn't yet seen his face. Unable to resist my need to take a quick peek, I snuck up to him.

At my first step, he wheeled toward me.

His gaze fell on me, so intense it froze me where I stood.

A swirl of dark stars came alive, brightening in his sapphire eyes.

"You came back," he said, his voice deep, silky, and rich, wrapping me with its potent seduction. I could orgasm just by listening to him talk a little longer. "I've been waiting for you."

A smile floated to my lips. "That's flattering, but I think this is the first time I've met you. Uh, do you have a name?"

Maybe I should also ask for his number and then get a phone.

"You don't remember me?" he asked.

My face sank a little. I would curse the universe if it had created such an utterly gorgeous man but made him a loony or a creep or something worse.

"Maybe you've mistaken me for someone else?" I asked before a new swirl of dismay swelled in my chest. If he mistook me for another girl, then I wasn't the one he was waiting for and eager to see. Then I had no business here.

He laughed sensually. "Come here, lamb. Last time we didn't get to talk." His laugh dropped, and his voice turned into dark silk. "Some force pulled you out of my dream too fast, and I wasn't pleased."

What he said didn't make sense. But then this was a dream, as he'd announced.

My body urged me to go to him, but I stood my ground and narrowed my eyes, still surreptitiously ogling him. "I'm not a lamb. You need to correct your mistake."

He sighed. "Fine, Marigold."

I sucked in a breath, happy that I wasn't the wrong girl who crashed this party.

The beautiful man rose from his chair as if impatient that I didn't move to him as fast as he'd demanded. Before I made another step, he'd reached my side. His arm lashed out and snuck around my waist.

The next moment, we were on the balcony with me in his lap and my shirt nowhere to be found.

This relationship had developed super fast. Before I even knew his name, I was already cuddled with him, topless.

"I can't wait to touch you again," he said, snuggling his nose against my neck as he inhaled my scent.

He smelled of clean male and dirty sex mixed with cinder and night. His scent caressed me, arousing me out of my mind.

I traced my fingers along the ridge of his defined muscles before I pressed my breasts against his hard chest.

I wanted to know how it felt to be skin on skin with him.

He chuckled in lustful amusement, his massive erection throbbing against my butt through his trousers. The near uncontrollable desire to tear his pants off and have his large, hard cock inside my heat assaulted me so hard I almost reached for his pants.

Wait a second!

I blinked, trying to regain some control. I didn't want to be perceived as a savage by this lovely man. Maybe I should slow down. But what if the dream ended abruptly before I could enjoy this man?

Yet I shouldn't be so willing and eager to get it on with a stranger like this, even in a dream, right?

"What's the matter, lamb?" he asked, genuine concern in his eyes. "You get this pouty look when you're worried. What's bothering you? You know you can talk to me."

My chest warmed. He wanted to talk instead of having his way with me right away, and he wanted to know my problems.

"I got into this new school by accident," I said, twirling his silky hair around my finger. "Everyone there knows their place and which house they belong to, except me. No one knows what I am or what kind of power I have. Everyone got their powers upgraded but I just got burned. I'm the freak."

I thought of all the runes dancing across my body, then disappearing under my skin, never to surface again, like golden coins falling to the bottom of the deep sea.

"Nonsense," he said, his sapphire eyes warm and loving. "You aren't any sort of freak. You're the woman of my dreams."

I gave him a bright smile with a genuine ease I never felt with anyone else.

"You have the best smile in the universe," he said, his thumb tracing my lower lip indulgently.

"I know," I said. "It's only for you."

He was the nicest dream man, and it was so easy to talk to him. If everyone in reality was even a little like him, the world would have more peace and less violence and death.

"I won't share you," he said. "You're mine."

Aha, my dream man was possessive, which wasn't going to work well since he couldn't have me outside of this dream. However, I didn't want to say anything that might upset him and spoil our beautiful moment.

"I don't even know if I have magic or not," I said. "Maybe I do, but it doesn't seem like it wants to be discovered. I don't blame it. I don't trust those people in the school either. They only want to turn me into a killer. That's all we are to them—killing machines." I untangled my finger from his hair and pressed my palm against his face.

He leaned into my touch, cherishing it.

His skin felt so warm, and his stubble pricked against the heel of my palm. This dream was amazingly realistic with all its scents and textures.

"The three big assholes who rule the school and half of the world can't figure out me or my powers," I babbled, grateful that he was still listening attentively. "I love how it frustrates them. They don't like mystery. They don't like the unknown. Yet I'll remain one, and that's my poetic justice."

"However," my grin waned, "I'm a bit concerned that if my power doesn't manifest soon, or if I'm really a dud, they'll have no use for me. They'll get tired of me and my attitude, and then they'll snap their thick, rude fingers and dispose of me. I bet one of them has already imagined erasing me from the face of Earth. I irked him pretty hardcore."

"No one will touch you," he snarled. "You're mine. I won't allow anyone to hurt you, even in a dream. I'll slay them all."

His wings whooshed out aggressively.

"Uh, thank you," I said. It felt nice that he was so protective of me, even it was in a dream. When it ended, he would disappear.

But then how come we both realized that this was a dream?

Wasn't that a bit bizarre?

Or maybe it wasn't a dream after all, but we'd met in an alternative universe?

Man, I didn't want to leave this realty. I didn't want to wake up from it.

"Thank you for listening to me," I said. "I've been whining a lot lately, which isn't my usual style. From now on, I won't bitch. Ever. I'll stay positive for you."

Mostly for my own sanity.

"That's my lamb," he said in approval as his eyes grew hooded from desire.

His mouth slanted onto mine.

He'd held back for so long to listen to my problems. A good man was rare these days, so I needed to cherish him.

But at this point, we both needed some hot, naked action.

His large hands roved over my sides, moving up my chest. I moaned against his lips when his palm cupped my swelling breast.

His tongue thrust through my parted lips, sweeping over my hard palate.

Pleasure buzzed all over me in tingling sensations.

My tongue caught his, tangling in an elegant, intriguing dance.

It felt so natural being with this gorgeous, winged being this way. Like we were meant to be together.

He let out a low groan, tearing his lips from me. His sapphire eyes shone brightly, filled with starlight. "You're the only woman I can touch, even in a dream," he said gently yet full of awe. "But even if I could touch another, I'd rather have you here in my dreams than any other woman in real life."

How could he have a real life? He was a fabricated character in my fantasy. But I had no time to dwell on logic while I was busy pulling him back toward me as I threaded my fingers into his lush hair.

I didn't want him to escape.

"Aren't you possessive and impatient tonight, lamb?" he chuckled, his voice husky and so sexy it sent liquid fire licking between my thighs.

"I want to touch you everywhere at once, lamb, and I don't even know where to begin," he said, his French accent thickening with lust. "You set my cock on fire."

Hell have mercy!

I crushed my lips against his.

Our tongues entwined, dueled, and danced.

A firestorm burned through us both, connecting us.

His hand moved down, tracing my warm skin. Pleasure stoked more flames within me at his every hungry stroke.

I rocked my ass against his erection.

A rough groan sounded from the back of his throat.

"I never knew touching a woman could be so delicious and addictive," he said. "You'll be my woman forever, lamb."

He heaved me up with one hand, and his finger rubbed my sex back and forth before sliding between my folds.

I leaned back to give him more room to play with me. Here in this beautiful dreamscape, I'd let him do anything to me.

His finger thrust slowly into me as he studied my reaction intently, like I was his new addiction—his whole world.

My inner walls clenched around his finger.

"It feels so good." I threw my head back and moaned. "And don't stop. Never stop."

He thrust deeper into me.

In and out and in with a smooth rhythm.

It didn't take long for him to insert a second finger into my tight channel and thrust more urgently.

I cried out as pleasure blasted through me, lighting up my every cell.

I wanted this mystical man more than anything.

I wanted his cock to replace his fingers so I could ride every inch of its hard length.

I propelled my hips forward to ride his fingers first, and he let out a string of lustful curses.

Unable to rein himself in any longer, the sexy hunk dropped his trousers, and I looked down at his cock—smooth, tanned, and huge. It was the most striking sight.

For a second, I hesitated. Would it fit? He was so big and I was tight.

I shook my head, determined not to worry about his size. We could make anything happen because everything could work in a dream.

I planted my hands on his shoulders and rubbed my sex along his hard length.

"Do you want my cock, lamb?" he asked.

He'd observed my every move in fascination, but the hungry way I stared at his manhood brought a smile of utter male satisfaction to his gorgeous face.

"More than anything," I purred breathlessly.

I hadn't known that I had this sultry side in me. I could be full of surprises, and this time it was in a good way.

An animalistic groan rumbled from his chest, arousing me even more.

His hands gripped my hips, lifting me up as if I were feather light. He placed his steel rod between my thighs and pushed me down.

I glided down and he thrust up, until we completely joined. We then remained still, savoring and celebrating this incredible feeling of intimacy and connection.

He started moving slowly, letting me adjust to his size.

I lost patience first. I wanted more of him—all of him. I heaved my hips up and down, sliding along his rock-hard length. I wasn't sure if I was doing it right, but it felt right, and we both panted in pleasure.

Bliss darkened his sapphire eyes, and unbridled lust twisted his face.

He gripped my hip with one hand as he thrust into me, faster and faster; his other hand buried into my lavender hair.

"Let me do the work and pleasure you, lamb." He breathed into my lips. "You just enjoy. I need to take care of you."

He bucked his powerful hips up and thrust deeper into me, his raw sexual need slamming into me, grinding me.

His every inch filled my heated channel, and my depths

swallowed every part of his manhood.

My breasts bounced up and down as we joined, parted for a second, and slammed back together.

A knot slowly unwound in me, and I only now realized that I'd been so tense for so long.

His lust, warmth, and scent wrapped around me like a melody from the sky, the ocean, and the depths of Earth.

He thrust into me, harder and faster, sending waves of pleasure washing over every part of my body. I wanted to cling to this sensation forever.

Another series of hard thrusts, and his cock grew even larger and harder inside me.

I moaned. He let out a low, guttural sound, his rhythm growing blindingly fast.

For a long moment, we didn't speak as he pounded into me relentlessly and I plunged from the tip to the hilt of him with equally bruising force.

"My woman, my lamb," he murmured, lust changing him, making him an erotic god. "You were made for me to find and pleasure in this pure ecstasy of my dreams."

"This is actually my dream," I said between breathless moans.

He ignored my correction and commanded. "Come to me in my dreams every night, lamb, and let me fuck you until dawn."

I squeezed him. My inner walls clenched every inch of his shaft.

He hissed in pleasure.

His velvet black wings came forward and wrapped around me in protectiveness and possessiveness as our rhythm became erratic with his accelerated thrusts.

Pleasure tossed me to the heavens, and something inside me completely loosened or snapped.

The glowing runes—all twelve of them, symbolizing the powers of the twelve major gods—swirled on my torso like a star chart of the galaxies.

I felt everything inside me—ice, wind, firestorms, lightning, harvest, death, birth, and darkness—racing to the surface.

It was chaos, then order, then chaos again.

I threw my head back as I pounded against him mercilessly.

Claim me. Take all I have.

I felt new. I felt like a whole new universe.

He stared at me in utter shock with his remarkable, sapphire eyes.

His sensual lips parted. "Marigold, what—"

A magical wind swept by, tearing me off him right before I climaxed in waves of wild passion.

"Marigold, wake up," someone called urgently.

CHAPTER 10

"What the fuck?" I flashed open my eyes and pushed down my flying fist before it rammed into Yelena's worried, kind face.

I groaned. "Damn, girl."

She'd just dragged me away from the sexiest man and hottest action with her terribly timed wakeup, and I'd been one breath away from having the first and best orgasm of my life.

Yelena's gray eyes stared down at me. "Class starts in twenty minutes, Marigold! You need to get up."

I sighed. She cared. She was a good friend.

"You go, pip," I told her. "I'll sleep just a little longer."

"Are you crazy?" she squirmed and flashed the class schedule in front of my one squinted eye.

8:00 AM: Cardio and weight training

9:30 AM: Olympian glory and history

10:30 AM: Combat techniques

12:00 PM: Lunch

1:30 PM: Weapons training

3:00 PM: Magic training

I was so not looking forward to any of those classes, especially after the dream I'd had. And for crying out loud, why should I give a damn about the Olympian gods' glory? Weren't they full of themselves?

"Our first class starts at eight," Yelena repeated. "It's seven-forty now. You don't want to leave a bad impression and start off on the wrong foot in a military academy, believe me."

What if I just missed a few classes? What was the big deal?

What could they do to me?

Kick me out of the Academy?

Peachy! That would be like a dream come true.

Thinking of dreams, I wanted more than anything to return to the one I'd been torn away from.

"Don't worry, pip." I lied. "You go, and I'll catch up with you. I'll get up in ten minutes, and I'll run all the way to class."

"Do you even know where the class is?"

"Like a map on the back of my hand."

She gave me one last uncertain, worried look. "Your face is all flushed. Are you okay?"

I pulled the blanket over my cheeks.

Yelena's footsteps retreated, and I glanced around to find that all the other girls had left before her.

Please, let me go back to that dream, I prayed to an imaginary higher force. *Let my dream lover wrap his black, silky wings around me one more time, and I'll promise to be on my best behavior for a week.*

I snuggled my nose deeper into the pillow.

Dream now, I commanded and hoped for the best.

I'd try anything to go back to him, to finish what we'd started, even though we'd have to say goodbye eventually.

I didn't find him.

I don't know how much time had passed when an icy dampness sank into my bones. Chunks of ice floated above my face, and the air was cut off from my water-filled lungs.

This wasn't the dream I sought.

I fought to breathe, to wake up, only to have more cold water pour into my mouth and down my throat.

Shit! Shit!

I snapped open my eyes, and to my horror, water flooded my bunk, encasing me like an ice coffin. This wasn't merely a bad dream.

Ice cubes floated above my face.

How could this happen in reality?

Was this an aftereffect of the ritual? I'd experienced the burn of the fire. Now must I freeze to death to finish the cycle? That ritual was a bitch!

I yelped for strength, threw the drenched covers off me, and leapt out of the soaked bed.

Then I realized I was completely naked, standing on my bare feet on the wet, cold ground.

I usually slept naked. Clothes irritated my skin.

"Now you're swift," Paxton said lazily, savoring the moment.

It all clicked.

Only the Demigod of Sea could pull this amount of water out of nowhere and force the currents to fly through the air like that.

I swept my furious gaze around the room and spotted him leaning against the column of a bunk. He wasn't wearing armor but dressed in a gray button-up shirt with black pants.

The Demigod of Sea might be sexy as fuck in the early morning, but I saw red, even though lust still lingered in my veins from the erotic dream. My anger spiraled higher when I registered that he enjoyed watching me shudder with cold.

He gave my nudity an intentionally slow once-over, meant to insult and irk me, yet he couldn't hide the heat in his violet eyes.

The weight of his intense gaze sent goosebumps all over my skin.

Instantly, I changed my strategy. Throwing a soggy pillow at him wouldn't do him any harm.

"Like the view?" I asked sweetly.

"You asked the same boring question at the ritual," he said. His gaze returned to my face after lingering on my breasts a bit too long. "What do you have that can possibly interest a demigod, mortal?"

"If you'll recall, your priest corrected you after the ritual. I'm not a mortal," I said, keeping my smile plastered on my face. "Should I expect a demigod to have short-term memory?"

If I wasn't a human, then what was I?

I hadn't had time or mental effort to attempt to sort it out. I only hoped that I wasn't some freak.

Spotting that fleeting hesitation and insecurity in my eyes, the demigod pounced.

"Then what are you?" he asked, arching an eyebrow casually.

I lifted my chin. It became an effort to keep the smile on my lips.

"Why should I tell you?" I asked as I staggered toward him, swaying my hips, instead of grabbing a sheet from my neighbor's bed to cover my nudity.

He tensed, straightened, and unfolded his arms from his muscled chest, which stretched his shirt deliciously.

"What are you doing, Marigold?"

"What do you think I'm doing?" I purred, letting a saccharine, sultry smile deepen the curve of my lips. "You should have known the answer when you charged into my personal space unannounced." I slowed down my tempo, still swaying my hips.

"Well, you can ask me to stop," I said in an easy challenge.

If he asked me to stop advancing on him or ducked away from my moves, then he was doomed to lose the first round.

He narrowed his violet eyes to cover the smoldering desire in them. He hated me, yet I had an effect on him, which made him hate me even more.

"You dare to challenge me again?" he asked.

I would do more than that, but I wasn't going to tell him that.

My smile grew sweeter. I was two feet from him now. I needed to get this over quickly. The syrupy smile on my face was getting old and cold and turning to yesterday's unpleasant leftovers.

A few inches from him, I raised my knee and rammed it toward his crotch, as fast and forcefully as I could.

Man, that would hurt! That would teach him a lesson about barging into a girl's dormitory while she was sleeping, working hard to find her dream lover.

For a nanosecond, an urgent, dreadful thought flitted through my head. What if his demigod cock was made of steel? Then it'd hurt me instead.

Before my knee found its mark, Paxton caught me, spun me, and pinned my back against him. His one hand grabbed both my wrists and held them against my belly, making my fingers dig into my skin. His other arm wrapped around my breasts, and his powerful legs had mine between them, so I couldn't kick him either.

He had me there, defenseless and furious.

I was faster than any human, but he was a demigod.

"That's the best you can do, Marigold?" he asked in mockery.

While I'd failed in my assault and was humiliated, I felt his huge erection against my back through his pants.

I could still get some reaction out of him. Maybe I should use that.

Then he twisted my wrists, and they hurt.

I blinked back sudden tears, and he loosened his grip a little.

"What are you doing here, barging into a girl's room?" I demanded angrily.

"This isn't a girl's room. It's a common dormitory. And as a student in my Academy, you don't have the luxury of privacy. I've received word that you missed physical training and also half of history class."

"Who ratted me out? Snitches get stitches!"

"You won't get revenge on anyone. The Academy has rules. For example, no one skips a class—among many others. You don't want to be late for class either."

"So *what* if I was late for a few classes?" I said. "I'm not a morning person. I like to sleep in. It's been my lifestyle for twenty years, and I'm not going to change it overnight."

"You *will* change your bad habits and attitude overnight. In fact, you'll change them now. You'll follow the rules like everyone else, and you'll learn discipline. If I have to beat it into you, I will. Try me and see who wins this game in the end. I look forward to our second round."

He shoved me away. I stumbled and nearly slammed my face into the façade of a cabinet between the bunk beds. I threw a hand out, grabbed an open drawer, and thus avoided a broken nose.

I wheeled toward him and hissed. "You fucker!"

"You have no fear, no respect, and no sense of self-preservation," he said, his face hard. "But I'll pound all those things into your skull in no time."

A sudden alarm buzzed in me. Axel had threatened that if I kept giving him headaches, he'd dole my punishments out to Jasper and Circe, knowing they were my weakness. What if Paxton had learned about my vulnerability? He wouldn't hesitate at all to exploit it.

I didn't wait for him to go there, just grabbed the sheet from Yelena's bed and wrapped it around my chest.

"Get yourself cleaned up and attend class," he said, steel in his voice. "You have three minutes."

"Where's Axel?"

"Miss him?"

"I'd take him over you any minute of the day," I said.

A muscle twitched in his jaw. I'd hit a nerve. It seemed there was a rivalry among the demigods.

"He isn't available, *Princesa*. You're stuck with me today."

"How tragic," I sneered. "Axel likes me. He'd have been more pleasant."

"He may be smitten with you for now. Even so, his father, the *god*, is more important than a simple girl like you. Ares summoned him to the city."

"Which city?"

"Paris, of course. Ares stays in Paris most of the time."

The unexpected response distracted me from my irritation. "I don't blame him," I said with longing. "I always wanted to go to Paris. I heard their crème brulee is top notch." I licked my lips. "I really want to try it someday."

"Like that's going to happen," he snorted, but he was looking at my lips.

I wouldn't put it past him to do his worst to take all the good fun out of my life.

"I heard Axel calling his father when the ritual went wrong with me," I pried.

"He did," Paxton said dismissively. "They have a mental link. But Ares was in the middle of a negotiation with Lucifer."

I'd once speculated that the God of War might have a dirty deal with the devil, or else how could Earth have been split so evenly into two evenly realms, one belonging to Ares and the other to Lucifer?

Politics were all dirty anyway. There were never good guys, only the lesser evil. And I still wasn't exactly sure which one was the lesser evil since I hadn't met either the god or the devil.

I arched an eyebrow. "Negotiation for what?"

The Demigod of Sea sent me a harsh look. "That's none of your business."

Probably not.

I shrugged just to irritate him. His gaze landed on my bare shoulders as if he wanted to remove the sheet from me and run his hands over my bare skin.

A shiver passed over me as heat rose between my thighs.

For a second, I must have looked confused. How could I still feel attracted to this demigod? He was an utter ass.

"Did Ares ever get back to Axel about the reason the ritual went awry with me?"

"Am I your messenger boy?" he hissed.

I sighed. As I'd said, an utter ass. But I didn't need this hostility so early in the day.

"What about Zak?" I asked hopefully. "He can't be away, too, right? He should have come to get me instead of you."

A dark light flashed through Paxton's eyes, turning the violet color to deep purple as the sea demigod grew angrier.

"Why am I even answering your questions?" he grated. "No one dares to question a demigod. No more stalling, Marigold. You're going to class, and you have two minutes left now. If you aren't ready by then, I'll drag you across the campus whether you have clothes on or not."

He wasn't kidding. He was ruthless.

I rolled my eyes, but I started searching for my name tag among the rows of drawers in the cabinet. My clothes should be inside one of these.

My mood was foul by the time I'd found the name Marigold, pulled open the drawer, and yanked out a uniform along with a pair of new boots.

I hoped that they got my size right, especially the shoes.

I didn't spare the demigod a glance as I took my uniform to the public bath chamber half a block away from my dormitory.

He didn't follow. I hoped that he'd leave while I changed.

For a second, I thought about running, but I gave up the idea before a plan formed.

I cleaned myself in record time, put on my uniform of blue and gray, and stood in front of a mirror before the sink.

I hadn't really looked at myself in a long time.

And now, a woman who hadn't completely lost the roundness in her cheeks stared back at me. She had elegant, long eyebrows that didn't need to be plucked into shape. Her lips were pink and full. Under her dark, thick eyelashes, her green eyes had the color of an untamed forest and the energy of a firestorm. There was so much life I stepped a pace back in shock.

"Marigold, look at you," I murmured to myself as I threaded my hand through my lavender hair.

I was still here. I lived. I hummed a tune, almost happy again.

"I've never seen a soldier that narcissistic," Paxton's voice commented as he suddenly appeared in the mirror behind me.

I hadn't noticed when he'd zoomed in.

"Are you spying on me in the women's bath chamber?" I asked, frowning at him deeply. "Do you even have a concept of boundaries, demigod?"

"I am above all rules and boundaries," he said arrogantly. "But you, the rest of you, are bound to all of them."

I wanted to toss something at the asshole, but I had nothing in hand. It wouldn't work anyway. He'd just give me a harder time. The Demigod of Sea sought to crush me.

As if he could hear my thought, his taunting gaze met my glare in the mirror, daring me to assault him.

"And what did I say about two minutes?" he asked.

"Sorry, mister," I said. "But I can't keep track of everything you said. You said a lot of things. Maybe you talk too much."

"Get going. Now."

I looked down. "I need to get my feet into my boots first."

Then I noticed that I was wearing a pair of mismatched knee-high socks.

"Wait," I said. "I need to change my socks."

"No, you don't," he said, stalking toward me.

He grabbed my ankle and roughly inserted my foot into the ankle-high boot, not even bothering to check first if the boot fit. But he got the job done. Then he snatched my other foot.

"Hey," I protested, laying a hand on his shoulder to keep my balance while he worked on getting my foot into the other boot. "My socks are different colors. Everyone will notice and laugh at me."

"I don't give a fuck if anyone laughs."

"Of course you don't give a fuck. I'm the one wearing them."

"If you embarrass yourself," he said, "you have only yourself to blame. And that will teach you a lesson about being timely and disciplined."

He stood up, grabbed my elbow, and dragged me out of the public bath chamber, not even giving me time to make my feet more comfortable in the new boots.

I stumbled alongside him.

"Hurry up!" he scolded.

"But I haven't had breakfast yet. Shouldn't I at least grab a cup of coffee somewhere or get a donut or two? I hope the Academy serves donuts."

"That reminds me," he said. "For your tardiness, you'll be punished by going without lunch. If you keep defying me, your dinner will be crossed out from today's activities as well. Whoever gives you food without my permission will be punished alongside you."

"That's unfair!"

"Welcome to Half-Blood Academy, Princesa."

He kept dragging me with him. The demigod walked so damn fast I had to sprint three steps to match one of his long strides.

"You should let me go," I said. "I can walk beside you with my own feet."

He snorted but maintained his hand on my elbow. I tried to shrug him off, but to no avail.

"Go ahead and fight me, Marigold, if you wish to take part in a public demonstration on how to punish an Academy student who doesn't know how to follow the rules."

I stopped cold. I didn't want any of that.

I didn't want any attention.

"You're just trying to find an excuse to touch me," I said. "Don't you think that's a bit desperate?"

"Nice try, Princesa," he retorted. "As if your words have any effect on me."

But my words had made him angry.

His jaw set as his dark eyes flashed. "I'll go easy on you only when you've learned to be respectful and behave in a civilized manner."

Dark fire swished in my eyes. The fucker demanded I have good table manners when he didn't even know what that was?

He'd pay dearly one day. But I wouldn't win against such a powerful asshole fighting him up close and personal. I needed to play dirty. I'd find a crack in him and then strike.

We reached the vast squares where the Dominion soldiers patrolled the campus. Groups of senior students practiced archery and magic in the training field.

They all paused in their activities to stare at Paxton and me, mouths agape. I supposed a student being dragged and manhandled by a demigod was a novelty on the campus.

No one dared to come to my rescue. My best hope, Axel, was thousands of miles away.

Paxton didn't even bother to glance around or acknowledge that everyone gawked at us.

Just great!

Now so many eyes had witnessed this. The whole Academy would soon know all about my humiliation. Demetra and her goons for sure were going to add salt to this wound.

I couldn't even snap at the asshole and tell him that I didn't like how everyone was watching him humiliate me. If I did, he'd exploit it.

No one loved public embarrassment. Not even me. So, I held my chin high, as if it were an honor to be dragged along by a demigod.

Finally we left the square behind and trekked down a corridor.

"Let me go, please, Demigod Paxton," I said in a low voice. There was no heat in my tone.

He gave me a look. "That's more like it." And he let go of my elbow.

That was his sick idea of taming me. He must have thought that he'd gained the advantage. All I wanted was to send my boot to his nuts, but I had tried that and failed.

We entered a classroom that could host at least two hundred students, but only fifty were present. My gaze swept over the surviving initiates, including Jack, Demetra, and their minions.

My predictable foes sneered at me.

Yelena grimaced, and Nat looked at me with sympathy.

The middle-aged professor in a black robe and broad hat immediately stopped preaching and bowed to his waist to Paxton.

"Demigod Paxton," he addressed. "It's an honor to have you grace my classroom."

"I brought you the student who tried to skip class, Fowler," Paxton said, as if I'd committed a cardinal sin.

I refrained from rolling my eyes. For crying out loud, it was just a class.

As if he sensed I'd mentally rolled my eyes, Paxton snapped his attention back to me, and I put on an innocent look. I didn't want him to go crazy right now in front of the entire class when I didn't have a backup, like Axel, or even Zak.

After this morning, I'd realized that this loose cannon had no brakes whatsoever. He was even worse than me.

Fowler probably thought the same, for he gave me an annoyed look, not understanding why a demigod would have bothered with insignificant me.

"If a student misses class, we usually give her a notice and put it in her record," Fowler said. "If she keeps up the offenses, we'll expel her from the Academy. Next time, I'll have a member from the Discipline Council serve her the notice. There's absolutely no need to involve a demigod like you to handle such a small matter, sir."

"Don't ever tell me how things get done again, Fowler," Paxton snarled. "Do you understand?"

As I'd said, a crazy on the loose.

Fowler paled, then stumbled back from the towering demigod.

"I apologize, sir," he said. "I didn't mean—"

"Professor Fowler meant that you're using a cannon to shoot a mosquito," I chimed in quickly and smirked at Paxton. I couldn't give up the chance to ridicule him, despite my decision to stop getting on his bad side in public. "I think he's spot on, though. There's really no need to bother yourself with an unimportant first-year like me, Demigod

Paxton, or sir. The Discipline Council can totally kick me out of the Academy after they serve me a few warnings."

"You're not getting out of the Academy under my watch," Paxton said vehemently and viciously. "So give up already, Marigold, or I'll make your life hell. Now wipe that disgusting, smartass smirk from your face. Your dinner rights today are also revoked."

He swept his stern gaze across the class, and everyone shrank in their seats.

My smile dropped. How was I going to get through the whole day without food?

"Anyone supplying Marigold with food can go on a fast with her for as long as it takes," Paxton added. "Understand?"

The entire class answered loudly, including the professor. "Understand!"

The clique giggled.

I didn't think Nat and Yelena also echoed that, but they had to move their lips to pretend, or they'd get punished, too.

"Good." Paxton said with satisfaction. "The Half-Blood Academy has decided to turn a ruffian like Marigold into a model soldier at all costs. She's our project now."

What the fuck?

"The Academy won't allow a delinquent to go on strike," he emphasized, watching my outraged expression like a fat cat regarding a cornered mouse.

Only I was no fucking mouse. He wanted a war, and he'd get one.

"Axel will never go along with that," I ground out, my eyes burning. "He's on my side."

"Is he?" Paxton said, a sadistic smile stretching his curvy lips. "Wasn't he the one who plucked you from the ghetto, dragging you from a bawdy street fight to the Academy, despite the way you begged and screamed for him to let you go? Wasn't he the one who was willing to see you die just to test if you could actually live through the ritual?"

I clamped my mouth shut, feeling like I'd been hit by a truck.

How naïve of me to even think that Axel and Zak might defend me just because they'd once shielded me from the burning fire.

They were all my enemies. They'd never been my allies. Paxton had just reminded me of that.

A cruel light glinted in Paxton's eyes at my devastated look. "Keep an eye on her," he ordered to no one in particular. "If she refuses to behave, if she sneezes wrong, call me right away."

Everyone nodded vehemently, especially the clique.

Paxton turned on his heel.

As soon as he showed his back, I flipped him the bird. I forced down my finger quickly, though, as I didn't want to be caught.

I grinned at the class sweetly. "Aren't you going to report it?"

The class gasped, but no one dared to call back the demigod. If they did, they'd have to repeat and mimic my vulgar gesture, and I didn't think Paxton would take kindly to being flipped off, even in demonstration.

He might be rough with me, but I knew he wouldn't kill me, not until he was utterly bored with me. And he wouldn't be bored until he bent me, broke me, and turned me into one of his herd.

Paxton strode away, whistling the tune I had hummed in the bath chamber.

Thankfully, the bell rang the next minute, announcing the end of the class. After all that, at least I didn't have to suffer through a lecture on the glory of the gods.

CHAPTER 11

We had a ten minute break before our next class: Combat Techniques.

Nat and Yelena sat with me on a wooden bench near a pond half-concealed by ancient trees. I was so hungry I really wanted to ask them if they had anything to eat, like an energy bar, a piece of chocolate, or something, but I didn't want to put them in a tough spot.

I couldn't ask them to smuggle out a sandwich or even an apple for me either, when they went for lunch. Paxton's people might be watching. And I knew the clique would keep an eye on me like a hawk to make sure I didn't get lunch.

"What happened?" Yelena said. "You said you'd get ready and run to class."

"Pigston is what happened," I said.

"Pig…ston?" Nat asked, a half-smile twitching the corner of his mouth.

"Yes, Pigston is Paxton," I said, "the one and the same."

Yelena glanced around nervously. "Shush, don't let anyone hear that," she whispered. "Demigod Pig—Paxton—will skin us alive if he ever learns about that name. He might really kill you with a snap of his fingers if you rile him up too much. I heard that the demigods have all killed over smaller offenses. Our lives aren't important to them, and they kill people without remorse."

"That's them," I said bitterly. "As you all heard today, I'm now their target. You two might want to stay away from me, too, or you might become targets as well." I gave them a rueful glance. "I cherish our friendship, but I don't want you to sink with the ship."

"No way," Yelena said. "We'll stick with you. We just hope you won't sink."

"We decided to take you under our wings that first day when you went up against Demetra, the One-eighth," Nat said, flashing me a warm, white smile.

Yep, he was a good-looking guy and very intelligent. At my appreciative look, he fumbled in his backpack and pulled out a bottle of water.

"Here," he said.

"No, no," I said, shaking my head. "Enemy spies could be anywhere. I won't let you lose your lunch."

"Demigod Paxton said no food," Yelena said. "He didn't say no water. But if you're really hungry, I'll get you a sandwich, no matter the consequences."

"Nope, pip," I said. "I'm not hungry at all. But water would be awesome. Our guy Nat can always find loopholes in their rules, and Pigston isn't too great with logic." I chuckled at my own joke, took the bottle from Nat, and drained half of the water. Then I grinned at my friends. "Thank you for not abandoning me."

"You have us," Nat said. "We'll watch your back when those bitches come for you."

For the first time since I'd come to the Academy, I didn't feel so alone anymore.

I still missed Jasper and Circe dearly. I didn't know if they fared well in the Other Academy or not, but I bet they couldn't do any worse than I was.

Rhiannon, a second-year from our dormitory, had mentioned that the next dinner where we ate with the Other Academy students would be in two weeks. She was dating a shifter who attended there, so she was looking forward to mingling with them as well.

"We gotta go," Yelena said. She never liked to be late for class.

After this morning, I didn't blame her. Thanks to that distasteful drama caused by the sea demigod, no one would dare test his patience by being late for class.

But shouldn't that asshole worry more about demons than me? No matter how rotten I was, I couldn't be worse than a demon, could I?

I hurried toward our combat lessons with Nat and Yelena. Combat sounded awesome. It'd be way more fun than weight training, running laps, and any bullshit about the Olympian whatever's glory.

At this point, I had loads of pent-up aggression, and I could use the class to legally beat the shit out of one of the clique snobs. Hopefully the teacher would pair me up with Demetra.

I could fight. I'd been a hunter.

We stepped into the training classroom in a low-rise, mauve building, and I noticed from my friends' wary expressions that I was way more eager than they were. The clique and all the other new initiates were already in the room, standing in front of the instructor, who turned out to be Lieutenant Cameron.

"I didn't expect that dude," I murmured to Yelena. "This isn't funny."

Marie was in the room as well, checking an assortment of weapons on the walls. It was the first time I'd seen her since the ritual.

I jogged toward her. Now that I'd survived, I needed to know where the Dominions had put my personal property—particularly the weapons they'd stripped from me in Crack. I needed them back.

"Hey, Marie," I called, smirking at her to warm her up.

She arched a wary eyebrow at me. "You got yourself into trouble again on your first day?"

"Me?" I asked innocently.

"I have ears everywhere, you know."

"So you say. You're the assistant instructor?"

"We rotate," she said, picking up a longsword from the wall and testing its weight.

"Better the devil you know," I said.

"Which devil?" she asked, then indicated her chin toward the entrance, and my smile sank.

Paxton strode into the room in a black T-shirt that displayed his huge biceps and cut chest. Loose trousers hung low on his hipbones.

Everyone bowed at the sight of the demigod, except me.

Involuntarily, I put a hand on my hip. Did he come to fight or seduce?

I got my answer quickly. All the girls' faces brightened up, even Yelena's. She only dimmed her smile when she spotted my sour look.

A demigod had that kind of power over everyone. It reminded me of how Axel had made everyone in the street kneel before him in Crack.

"What the fuck is the swimming boy doing here," I whispered to Marie while she was still bowing. "He shouldn't be here, right? Shouldn't he go fight demons and protect humanity instead of idling around the training hall and harassing poor initiates?"

I had a bad feeling that he'd come for me.

I didn't want him to be here. I didn't want him to be anywhere near me.

Marie held back a laugh and whispered back. "Do not talk to me during the training. You're a bad influence, and I don't want to go down with you. You might have caught the eye of the Demigod of War, but I've got no one to watch my six."

Paxton had made me a pariah in the Academy.

The assistant instructor sent me a pitiful, pained look. "The demigods have never trained students anywhere, let alone the initiates. They typically don't stay at any Academy for more than three days, and the four of them usually don't stay in the same place. Everyone knows how territorial they are."

She blew out a breath. "I think they're all going to stay at this Academy for a while because of you. No one has any freaking idea why the divine flame chose you and why you have no icon from any of the gods' houses. The demigods don't like dark secrets and mysteries. Congratulations, Marigold, you've become their new obsession."

I raised my eyes toward the ceiling as if praying to a god like a pilgrim. "Oh, spare me, great ones. I'm not a freak. I was just misfortunate enough to be in the wrong place at the wrong time."

"Very mature, Marigold," she said. "But I'm still offering you my last piece of advice: let them get bored with you so they'll shift their attention somewhere else. Tread carefully. Half of the world is theirs, and you can't win—no one can—if you go up against them."

I hadn't gone up against them, against any of them, but one of them had come to my world and ripped me from the life I'd chosen for myself. But Marie wouldn't understand my point.

She snuck away, not wanting Paxton to think that she and I might be tight.

Cameron clasped his hands and called sternly. "Class, all in."

All seven initiates, now the first-years, snapped into two lines before the Dominion lieutenant. I strolled toward them, ignoring Paxton's gaze on me. It might be best for me not to acknowledge his presence. At all.

Cameron started his clichéd opening speech with, "This is the class of basic combat training, your introduction into a great career as a Dominion soldier."

I almost raised a hand and asked him what if I didn't plan to be a career Dominion soldier. I knew it wasn't up to me, though. Half-Blood Academy had said clearly that I couldn't turn down its summons, but I still couldn't help rebelling against how they'd robbed me—all of us—of our freewill. Then again, maybe the whole idea of freewill was a delusion.

"Here, you'll learn the traditions, strategies, and techniques to become a Dominion soldier," Cameron continued. "You'll learn discipline as we instill in you the codes and creeds of the Academy. You'll accomplish tasks. After you graduate from this class, you'll move to advanced combat training, where you—"

"We're going to make a few adjustments," Paxton cut in impolitely, his voice booming. And every student, except me, wheeled toward him as if he were a god.

I almost shouted at them that Pigston was only a demigod. And I wondered why Cameron didn't even protest as he was basically shoved away. The lieutenant was the rightful instructor, but he just stepped aside silently.

"We'll skip the out-of-date procedures," Paxton said. "Basic training is no longer practical in today's world. We've lost a lot of strong, disciplined soldiers fighting the good war against the demons. We need many more capable soldiers. We need you to step up and be battle-ready. As a result of my discussions with my demigod peers and the generals yesterday, we have decided that from now on, Half-Blood Academy will be a two-and-a-half year program instead of dragging on for four years. All of you will follow a new curriculum."

The fucker changed the rules just like that.

Cameron and Marie traded a subtle look. They weren't in the loop either.

"Let's start with learning your strengths and weaknesses," Paxton continued, his hard gaze falling on me.

What had I done now? He just couldn't take his gaze off me, could he? But I restrained myself from pulling my lips back to a half-sneer. So I half-turned to him and half-listened. Marie had warned me not to be a fool hitting a rock with an egg, but I could be a hard-boiled egg.

"I'm going to pair you up and get you started," Paxton continued. "Let's see what kind of material you're made of."

A human material? I mouthed.

So the Demigod of Sea wanted to get us fighting right away. He was even more bloodthirsty than his Demigod of War cousin.

That was fine with me so long as he didn't pair me up with either Yelena or Nat. I didn't want to hurt them.

So when Paxton sent Nat to fight George, the other outsider, I beamed. But when he called Yelena and Demetra, I stepped forward.

"I volunteer to have a bout with One-eighth in Yelena's place," I said.

"One-eighth?" Paxton asked, narrowing his eyes, and Demetra shot daggers at me, face reddening in anger.

"Oh, sorry," I said. "I meant Demetra."

Cameron kept a straight face. Marie coughed over a chuckle, then covered her mouth and shot me a warning glance. The other students stared at me in shock, but one of them chortled shortly.

"Did you know we have a rule of no name-calling in Half-Blood Academy, Marigold?" Paxton asked.

"Which clause?" I snickered since I bet he'd made that up just now.

"Quote it, Cameron," Paxton said.

"Half-Blood Academy Dominion Soldiers' Code of Conduct number 1175 says—" Cameron started, but Paxton waved him off.

Damn! There were over a thousand codes of conduct? I blinked in shock and dismay. How was I going to navigate them all?

"For your violation of Half-Blood Academy Dominion Soldiers' Code of Conduct number 1175, you'll receive another punishment," Paxton said. "You can run twenty laps during lunch since you won't be eating today."

So he not only wanted to starve me but also planned for me to pass out running twenty laps on an empty stomach.

"Give me a break," I said, planting my feet apart. "You called me a name, too."

The class gasped at my audacity. Yelena and Nat looked really worried now. Marie shook her head at me.

"What did I call you, Marigold?" Paxton asked in mocking curiosity.

I wouldn't take the bait. He knew I hated it when he called me *Princesa*. I wasn't going to say it aloud and have the whole school calling me that.

"You know exactly what you called me," I said. "It came out of your mouth."

"Thirty laps now," Paxton said. "And you won't fight Demetra. I'll give you Jack."

I eyed the biggest guy in the class. He was like a year older than me. Judging from his size and muscles, I'd bet all my money that he ate, slept, and shit in the training room.

That jackal grinned at me malevolently.

He'd wanted to beat me up for a while, and a bigger villain had just granted his wish.

I pulled my lips back and flashed him a vicious grin as well.

"What weapons can we use?" I asked.

I was a weapon girl. Giving me a bow, a sword, a spear, anything, and I was golden. I'd found one that would give me the upper hand while I'd talked to Marie by the wall of weaponry.

"You won't fight with a weapon," Paxton said firmly. "The match will be hand-to-hand combat."

My heart dropped to my stomach.

I'd never trained in fist fighting or wrestling. I didn't like strangers touching me in any way, including in a street fight. Paxton must have known that I was good with weapons, so he'd stripped me of my advantage.

"If we have weapons, why would we want to use meaty fists?" I protested. "We aren't going to win against demons by throwing a few meek punches here and there. It's better to behead the demon fuckers with sharp blades. So I say Jackie and I go for a weapon match, unless he's too chicken to lift a blade."

The room hushed to complete silence.

What? They didn't like me talking like a truck driver?

"Now you're the instructor?" Paxton snarled. "One more word and you'll be running forty laps."

The clique sniggered, and Demetra giggled as she sent the Demigod of Sea a sultry, adoring gaze. But he wasn't looking at her. He was too busy glaring at me.

The fighting ring formed quickly.

Nat went against George first. They were nearly the same height and build. Both good-natured guys threw a few punches at each other and delivered a variety of kicks.

No one got hurt, and then the fight was over.

Paxton waved them aside, calling it a tie.

I bit my lip, watching everyone's moves as I calculated potential counterattacks against Jack. He was double my size, so I had to avoid any direct hits. I couldn't allow him to pin me down either.

Once his dead weight was on me, I'd be done with.

Yelena charged Demetra as soon as they were both in the ring. After a few punches, they ended up grabbing each other's hair. Demetra got the upper hand. She gave Yelena a black eye as she dragged my friend to the ground by her ponytail, shrieking in joy like a harpy the whole way.

Unable to watch quietly, I threw my friend an instruction. "Roll to your left and kick the nasty she-beast's fucking teeth."

But Yelena was too obsessed with making her foe bald to listen to advice. Cameron had to break them up after both girls kept tearing strands of hair from each other's scalps.

And then it was my turn. I spared a remorseful glance at a wicked dagger hanging vertically on the wall.

That asshole Paxton wouldn't cave. He wanted to see me fall more than anything. He didn't allow me to have my boots on either, which I'd thought about using as a weapon at some point. The heels were hard, and with good aim, I could thrust them into Jack's eyes to get him off my back if he ever got me in a bind.

I also stripped off the socks of different colors. I'd gotten plenty of snickers and giggles behind my back and to my face all morning.

Nat and Yelena glared at Jack because they dared not glare at the Demigod of Sea for the unfairness of the match. They were brave and loyal enough to stay friends with me and show me support. Others would have ditched me at the first sign of the demigod's displeasure toward me.

Hadn't Marie warned me not to talk to her?

Everyone was afraid of Paxton, even the Dominion lieutenant.

Jack swaggered to the ring first, as if he owned every inch of it, his vulture-like eyes dwelling on me. The look said he was debating where to land the first strike and break my bones.

"There'll be no rules in the fight," Paxton said. "It ends when someone yields."

The demigod hadn't said a thing about yielding when the other pairs went against each other. And Cameron always stepped in before the fight went overboard.

But now Paxton was warning the instructors to stand by and giving his pawn a license to kill me. There'd be no consequences if Jack beat me to death.

Cameron's face remained stony, but a dark worry flitted through Marie's eyes.

They knew Paxton was using the fight to set me as an example and to crush my spirit and break my will.

All eyes fixed on me. Every first-year had also realized that the Demigod of Sea had marked me.

Jack's malicious, superior grin grew wider as he got the message, proud as a peacock that he'd become the demigod's executioner.

I bet Paxton knew all about Jack's capabilities. The Academy had everyone's file.

Demetra sent Paxton another worshipping gaze and clasped her hands. "Take her down mercilessly, Jack. Give her the Hell she deserves. That harpy doesn't belong in the Academy."

While Jack was the demigod's weapon, Demetra was his most vehement cheerleader. What a diabolical lot.

And why weren't the instructors quoting school codes now that she was calling me names?

As soon as I stepped into the ring, my fear left and rage rose as I met the sinister promise in Jack's eyes. He looked at me as if I wasn't a person but his victim. He'd beat me within an inch of my life before killing me to please and impress the demigod.

"Hey you, douchebag," I called, eyeing Jack like he was born from a rattlesnake.

He probably was, though he didn't hiss half as loud or venomously as Paxton.

"You know you're just a pathetic pawn in some asshole's petty personal agenda to bring me down, right?" I asked. "And I have bad news for you. I won't go down easily."

I wanted them to know I was well aware of what they wanted to do to me and I wasn't afraid. I'd dealt with plenty of killers in my hunter years back in Crack.

Paxton's violet eyes turned dark purple, anger and the threat of punishment brewing in them.

The instructors and the students shifted their feet nervously. No one dared to openly challenge a demigod, and anyone calling one an asshole in public wouldn't normally be allowed to breathe again.

I dared. He was going to kill me anyway, so I might as well get mouthy to get back at him, even though it was but a small, sad revenge.

I hated it that it was always assholes and mass murderers ruling the world. I hated it that it was always the little people and the innocent who suffered.

How I wished there was something I could do to fix that harsh reality, but the idea of changing the world was ridiculously impossible. I might not even survive this stupid brawl.

"Get on with it," Paxton barked, his cold voice fuming.

I stretched my neck and flexed my shoulders to rile him up, defying him at every turn while I still could. Jack, though, didn't wait. He launched at me like a remorseless bull with the determination to hurt and maim me.

I sidestepped at the last second, deploying my best asset—speed.

I ducked a heavy-weighted swing from my opponent and lashed out with my foot toward the back of the punk's knee.

To my surprise, he didn't even bother avoiding my kick. He threw his elbow toward my exposed throat just as my foot connected with his knee.

He didn't go down, not as I'd expected. He took the blow easily without even bending his knee.

It dawned on me instantly.

He must have been training for the role of Dominion soldier since he could walk. He'd known he was a descendant of the gods. Most people considered being a part of the gods' army the greatest honor, even though Half-Blood

Academy was not-so-secretly called Half-Death Academy by some dissidents.

And a new reality sank in—I wasn't faster than Jack.

I'd gotten used to being faster than anyone else in my hunter years, but that advantage had ended just now.

While the Ritual of Blood Runes hadn't done anything for me, other than burned me brutally and marked me as an uncategorized freak, all the other initiates who had survived the ritual had gotten way more powerful.

The powers granted to them because of their bloodline had all manifested.

They'd become faster and stronger, a better version of themselves, as befitting a student of the Half-Blood Academy.

That moment of distraction and bitter feelings cost me instantly when Jack drove his fist toward my head. I leapt back to dodge the jab, but I wasn't quick enough. Though he missed my skull, his blow smashed onto my shoulder blade.

I widened my eyes in astonishment as I heard the clear, sharp sound of my bone cracking. Pain jolted throughout me, threatening to paralyze me. But I couldn't allow that, or I'd be done with before it even started.

My opponent was stronger than I'd thought. He was no longer a mere human male. He'd upgraded. He was now formally a part of the killing machine, a strong descendant of the Olympian gods, while I remained the non-evolved.

If his fist had smashed into my head, he'd have opened my skull.

A flick of surprise also passed through his expression, twitching a muscle in his jaw. He hadn't expected me to be fast enough to dodge his killing strike.

The rumor on campus, probably started by Demetra and her minions, was that I was a dud because I wasn't a true descendant.

Jack probably thought that eliminating me was doing me a favor; he definitely thought it was what the Demigod of Sea wanted.

Though my shoulder throbbed, I pushed through my shock and agony so I could spin out of the next series of jabs, punches, and dropkicks from my adversary. In the meantime, I blocked out the clique's cheering for their champion.

With a weapon, I might be able to show him what I was capable of. But the demigod had known that and pitted my weakness against my opponent's strength. I hadn't the slightest edge over Jack. Even his weaknesses seemed stronger than my strengths.

We circled each other. He attacked and I parried, taking a few more hits on my sides and one on the jaw as I observed his moves, desperate to locate his Achilles' heel.

I wasn't familiar with boxing, which seemed to be Jack's favorite sport. I bet he'd have been a pro boxer if he hadn't been accepted into the Half-Blood Academy.

He swung his thick arm toward my face while his other hand tried to ram into my middle, intending to punch out my breakfast.

Unfortunately for him, I hadn't had any, but I was wise and just fast enough to leap out of harm's way.

When he aimed his next punch toward my ear, hell-bent on damaging my eardrum, I ducked from under his arm and rammed my fist into his side, as hard as I could.

He didn't even flinch. He was built and trained for hits and impacts much heavier than my puny fist could deliver.

I couldn't do any damage to him without a blade.

And I had no magic.

After a few bouts, he'd cracked my shoulder blade and a rib or two, yet I still stood, still fought back as viciously as I could, despite how badly I was outmatched.

It was getting hard to keep pushing through the agony my every muscle and bone felt from the brutal onslaught of my opponent. Luckily, instead of shutting down, my body still coordinated with my commands.

Maybe I was just too stubborn.

Jack marched toward me, and I staggered back.

A defensive strategy no longer served me when I was facing a stronger and faster foe. I now met him blow for blow. Every time my knuckles whacked him, pain radiated to my arms and shoulders. I started to suspect his muscle really was hard as rock, or maybe he'd used his enhanced power, boosted by the runes, to harden his muscles.

I wouldn't know how it worked since I hadn't gotten any fucking benefit from the ritual.

I'd started bleeding everywhere and pain throbbed through my every fiber.

Everyone watched Jack pound me like a lion on a housecat. The clique cheered every time their champion thumped a new punch on me.

"Maul her face again!" Demetra shouted instructions. "Make her ugly."

Paxton didn't make a sound, but I could picture the sadistic, satisfied smile plastered on his face at the pathetic, helpless sight of me.

That was what he wanted.

I must have looked really wretched, because both Nat and Yelena started calling out, despite their fear of the demigod.

"Yield, Marigold!" Nat shouted.

"Marigold, please yield," Yelena pleaded. "Let's fight another day."

There was no other day. I wouldn't give the fuckers that satisfaction.

They could make me yield over my dead body.

Jack kicked me in a devil-style, faster than my swollen eye could catch. The hard heel of his foot rammed into my left ear.

A new layer of pain blossomed in my head, and my ears felt like I'd been hit by a train.

For a few seconds, all I could hear was the unbearable ringing that pounded my ear, drowning out the cheers, begging, and curses from my classmates.

Yet I still heard Paxton's scolding, "You think this is the worst you'll face, Marigold? You'll face far worse. The demons will do more terrible things to you when they catch you if you're as sloppy as this."

Oh, I'd rather to be caught by the demons than by the demigods, fucker! But I had no strength or time to tell him that before Jack lunged at me again.

This time, I dodged faster than he'd expected me to be able to, as rage pumped through my veins.

I swept his legs from under him. He fell to the ground with a thud, and I leapt on him, my balled fist colliding with his cheekbone.

I heard a crack.

His face was his weakest spot.

I wasn't useless after all. Accustomed to his combat style, I was getting better.

But I was too wounded. I believed that I had internal bleeding as well.

I straddled him, and jammed my fist into his eye socket. He caught my wrist, twisting it, and at the same time he pushed up with a stupid yell and threw me off.

I ended up beneath him.

I kicked out right away. And just like before, my kicks and punches didn't have much effect on his person.

His heavy fist docked on my face again and again, shredding my skin and breaking bones. Blood flowed hot and free from my torn skin.

I was going to look really ugly if I survived this.

"Beg, bitch," he hissed in my ear. He straddled me with his knees digging into my chest, sadistic pleasure written all over his face. His hands gripped my wrists, bruising my skin, and he pinned them to my sides. "Beg and I'll consider not breaking another weak bone of yours. I might even let you live. Admit you're my bitch now, and I'll go easy on you."

He'd broken my body, just as his master, the Demigod of Sea, wanted.

I struggled to throw him off me, but his weight felt like a thousand pounds.

"Want to be on top?" He leered at me.

"Hi, Jackie," I said.

He blinked at his nickname.

Taking advantage of his diversion, I butted my head into his nose, crushing it into a grotesque mess. Two trails of blood streamed down from his nostrils. As I'd discovered, his face was his only weakness.

"You don't look that pretty anymore," I chuckled.

"Bitch! You don't deserve mercy," he said, pounding a fist into my teeth.

My tongue tasted a mouthful of salty blood. Pain radiated in every corner of my head as if a thousand horses had kicked my skull. It was a wonder I hadn't passed out or died already, but then I was Marigold, the most stubborn hunter in Crack before they'd dragged me here.

I hadn't groaned once, despite that I could no longer block out the pain as it filled my every bone marrow.

I laughed, mocking my opponent when he rammed his fist into me again.

What else could he do to me?

He cursed when I bit into him and tore a chunk of flesh from his thick arm.

"Stop, please." Yelena stated crying and knelt before the demigod for me. "Please just ask him to stop. He's killing her. She won't last long."

"Yield, Marigold. Now," Paxton command.

"Fuck you, pig!" I answered.

I knew that insult to the demigod would do me in. Who the fuck cared? I'd call him whatever I wanted.

"We should call off Jack, sir," Cameron said urgently. "That stupid, bull-headed girl will never yield."

"Please, sir," Marie said. "I don't think it's in your best interest to kill her off so soon. I believe she's learned her lesson."

"Jack," Paxton called, a regretful note in his voice, "you can—"

His mercy was the last fucking shit I'd take. And hearing the emotion in his voice only sent me right to the edge.

Something primal and savage in me was suddenly set loose.

I roared my black rage.

A wave of energy blasted out of me in light and shadow, tearing Jack away from me and tossing him to the arched ceiling, as if he were a rag doll.

The concrete dented at the impact.

Jack screamed before he plummeted to the ground in a corner. He didn't move again.

One strike and he was out.

"What a pussy," I murmured.

"What the hell was that?" someone asked in alarm.

I struggled to rise to my feet. Once I got there, I swayed but I remained upright. "That's called never *surrender*, bitches," I said, spitting out a broken tooth along with a flow of blood.

Then I flipped both middle fingers at the Demigod of Sea as my stare fixed on him. "You'll never bend me. You'll never break me. And you'll never get the best of me. So why don't you get your demigod head out of your ass, since all you'll ever get is the nightmare version of me, dickhead."

"No one has ever called me that many nasty names," he growled. "I can squash you like a bug with a snap of my fingers."

I chuckled to deride him.

Damn! It hurt to move any piece of any muscle.

"Whatever," I said. "I'm not afraid of you. I'm not afraid of death."

"There are worse things than death, Princesa." His tone was dark, but there was weariness to it, as if he knew what he was talking about. Like I gave a shit at this point.

"Bring it on, motherfucker," I said. "You marked me as your enemy, and today I also marked you as my foe."

"We'll see about that," he said, muscles twisting in his jaw and storms wheeling in his purple eyes. "We'll see how you make me your enemy."

I spat. I wished he was closer so I could spit my blood into his cruel fucking face.

"Even if I can't strike you down," I smirked at him, "I pray that Lucifer will do it for me one day."

That was the ultimate blasphemy. But I wanted to defy him down to my every bone, and I wanted him to know it before he impaled me, murdering me with his power. He could easily summon an ice spear from the air and pierce my heart.

To my shock, my undiluted hatred for him made him flinch.

"However," I said. "Patience isn't my strong suit, so I won't wait for Lucifer and his legion to beat your ass."

Despite the excruciating pain throbbing through me, I remained articulate.

I threw up my hands, calling for my awakened magic.

My energy blast had probably sent Jack to the netherworld, so it should do some considerable damage to the asshole who stood six yards away from me.

"You dare to fight me, Marigold?" he asked lethally, remaining every bit in control.

"Not to fight you," I said softly. "To kill you."

My blood boiled inside me at the call of war.

Twelve runes rose to my skin, twirling up on my neck and slithering up my face.

"It's impossible," Cameron said. "She's got all twelve powers."

Nothing was impossible. I'd just proved that.

"Calm down, Marigold," Marie called. "Please calm down. Don't do anything you'll regret later. Let's talk about this."

"Talk? After all this, you want to fucking talk?" I laughed without mirth. "And regret isn't in my vocabulary."

I could feel my eyes glowing. The last thing I wanted was to calm the fuck down.

"Let her come to me," Paxton said. "Let's see what she's got."

My power rose.

It wasn't lightning, water, air blast, or any of the powers from the twelve houses of the Olympian gods whipping around me.

A sheet of dark crimson fire, more like hellfire, surged toward the demigod.

"Burn him to Hell!" I howled.

Solid ice walls formed around Paxton and the rest of the class. The demigod sent the storm of his icy current crashing into my fire.

The impact of the two opposite forces sent shockwaves all around and tore through the ceiling.

Concrete, dirt, and rocks rained down with water and ice. Pieces of wood caught fire and flew in all directions.

The students scattered as fast as their feet could carry them, staying clear of Paxton and me.

I pushed my fire toward the demigod, my body trembling from the strain.

But my flame grew weaker.

I realized in dismay that I had no more magical juice left, just throbbing pain in my core. Embers of my fire sparked then smoldered as they died on my fingers.

The Demigod of Sea called off his storm.

I wobbled, waiting for the demigod to strike me down. My hands stretched like claws, ready to leave a trail of blood on his face when he came to me.

Instead of murdering me, he turned to Marie and ordered, "Call the healers. Now."

Just then, Axel and Zak charged into the training hall, their gazes sweeping to me in utter shock.

I grinned at them savagely. I was but a standing, bloody meat pulp.

"What the bloody hell?" Zak thundered. "Who hurt her?"

Axel's fiery eyes scanned the room, looking for threats, before alighting on me again.

"Who touched my Marigold?" he roared in rage.

My vision blurred as black dots danced before my eyes. I'd held on long enough. I still fought to stay conscious, though I'd now welcome a break from the unceasingly excruciating pain pounding in my skull, in my every cell.

I don't know if Zak or Axel reached me before I fell on my face.

CHAPTER 12

As if I was floating above my body, I saw myself curled up on the ground, my lavender hair spilling around my gory face. My left cheek split open, as were my lips. My left eye was a black circle and my right one a patch of swollen red.

I was a grotesque sight, but all I felt was a cold, detached emotion.

I must have died.

As I peered at myself more closely, I noticed that though broken, I was wrapped inside some kind of a protective bubble made of pale crimson light.

Axel, Theodore, and a healer crouched outside the orb.

None of the students were in the room. It was just the demigods, the priest, the healer, and me—my body and my ghost.

Axel touched the boundary of the bubble, and a slew of crimson lightning shocked him, throwing him back.

"None of us can take down her force field," Theodore said. "We'd better stop trying and wait for her to wake up."

"How could she erect such an orb in such a state?" the healer, a dark-skinned mature woman in her thirties, murmured as she put a healthy distance between herself and the bubble.

"Her magic must have kicked in and created it to protect her," Zak said.

He was facing off against Paxton to prevent him from getting near me.

"We need to get her shield down, or she'll bleed out," Axel said, devastation and grief in his dark-golden eyes.

"We don't want to force it down and hurt her," Zak said, one hand rubbing his temple, the other up in the air to fend off Paxton. "We need to call Héctor back. He's an expert on shielding."

"Let me try it," Paxton said. "I might be able to bring down her shield so our healer can fix her."

At the sound of his voice, all my emotions wheeled back. My hackles rose, my skin prickled, and cold hatred burned through me.

"Fuck off, Paxton," Zak snarled. "You have no rights to her anymore."

"Don't let that fucker get one inch closer to her," Axel bellowed. "I'll have a word with him after I make sure Marigold lives. He's started a war this time."

"The hell I'll let any of you kick me out of the game," Paxton said. "She's mine as much as she's yours."

Game? What kind of sick game was he talking about? Were the demigods all playing a game with me? How dare that psychopath think I was his? Did he have an ounce of fucking common sense?

"After what you did to her?" Axel hissed in wrath.

"You've gone too far, Paxton," Zak agreed, regarding the sea demigod like an icy statue. "You don't deserve a mate like her after you laid your hands on her—after you encouraged another student do this to her. We never hurt our own. There's no coming back from this for you."

"I never meant for this to happen," Paxton growled. "I didn't expect her to be so bullheaded. I've never met anyone as stubborn, hot-headed, and infuriating as her. She refused to yield, and it got out of control. I was about to stop it. I just wanted to see what she was made of, what made her tick, and how much she could take so I could bend her a little. Our girl has a short fuse and a hotter temper. So it backfired, all right. I'll fix it."

"Fix it, my ass!" Axel said. "Look at her. Look what you did to her. You crossed the line, you sick fuck! She's not your girl, and you'll never touch her again."

"You don't get the final say in our pact, cub," Paxton said coldly. "We've found the one woman for us all, and I won't back off. I'll have my share. And for your information, she hates you, too. She knows exactly what you've done to her. You dragged her to the Academy and risked her life in the ritual for your own curiosity."

"I knew she'd survive!" Axel shouted.

"But she didn't know that," Paxton sneered. "You aren't on better ground than I am. She didn't just declare war on me; she declared it on all of us. If I can't have her, neither can you."

"You bastard!" Axel snarled. "You ruined everything. If she doesn't live, I'll kill you with my bare hands."

"Bring it on, cousin," Paxton said. "I'll take you down first and have her all for my own."

The Demigod of War wheeled from the orb that encased me, wrath radiating off him, and charged the Demigod of Sea.

The two demigods crashed.

Kicks and punches flew as they pounded each other without mercy. The brutality of their fight would've shocked me before, but not after today.

"Enough!" Zak shouted.

The priest and the healer darted nervous glances between the battling demigods.

I put a few things together.

I wasn't dead.

Those assholes were fighting over me. They wanted to make me theirs, even after what they'd done to me.

They thought they could just take whatever they wanted.

I needed to get out of here. I needed to stay as far away from those psychopaths as possible.

I slammed back into my body, and the returning pain blasted through my every muscle, bone, and tissue.

I suppressed a scream as my eyes fluttered open.

Axel and Paxton were still engaged in their mêlée. Zak tried to break them up and rammed fist after fist toward Paxton's face.

"Marigold?" The healer noticed my stirring first and called, "Marigold, can you hear me?"

I flicked a glance at her and frowned.

"You're injured badly, Marigold," Theodore stuttered, as if surprised that I'd returned to consciousness. "You need to lower your shield so Melissa and I can heal you." He paused for a second and added, "You're safe now."

The fuck I'd let anyone come near me or touch me. All I wanted was to get out of here.

But I couldn't move an inch. My broken body wasn't cooperating.

So I begged my magic to do something for me.

When I attempted to summon it, my power answered.

An incorporeal and nearly liquid flame coursed through me, soaking me—not to burn me but to heal me. Every place it touched and licked, it healed.

My tissues and bones started to knit together, mending and repairing themselves rapidly.

The pain ebbed inch by inch.

Melissa widened her eyes. "My gods, she's regenerating faster than a demigod."

Zak, Axel, and Paxton halted their onslaught and rushed toward me.

I wouldn't let them come to me. I was so done with all of them.

But where could I go?

In my desperate hour, I thought of the sweet, erotic dream I'd had this morning before the Demigod of Sea charged into my dormitory and started this charade.

I thought of my winged, beautiful dream lover and how I rode him to the heavens.

If only he were real.

If only I could meet him in the real world.

Wouldn't I give half of my soul for that?

I rose into the air, my body going as incorporeal as my spirit had been.

"Marigold!" Axel screamed. "Don't leave."

His fingers, warm, desperate, and possessive, brushed over my fingertips like a phantom touch before I faded from the room and disappeared.

CHAPTER 13

It was said that no students could teleport out of the warded Academy, but I defied their textbooks once again.

No walls could confine me.

It turned out that I had magic that was possibly more powerful than any descendant of the Olympian gods possessed, except for the demigods.

Why hadn't it come out before Jack had beaten me to within an inch of my life? It had come through in the end, so maybe I shouldn't complain much.

Maybe my power needed a trigger to manifest?

That Pigston was right about one thing, I wasn't disciplined. I didn't know how to master my magic, so it appeared as unruly as I was.

It was volatile. It connected to my emotions, especially my rage, but I couldn't always depend on my anger to bring out my power.

I needed training to effectively wield my magic, but I would never return to the Academy.

What if I found myself a remote place, holed up in it, and learned about my magic on my own?

I surveyed my new surroundings before trotting down an abandoned street, a feeling of déjà vu washing over me.

I'd once passed by this street, but I couldn't remember when and with whom. I still had missing years in my broken memory bank that I couldn't decode.

Those years were locked, just as my magic had been caged until the Ritual of the Blood Runes had somehow broken the seal on the well of my power.

Images flashed before my eyelids like old, fading pictures, and instantly I knew this avenue used to be the block between Manhattan's Chinatown and Little Italy. One street separated two completely different cultures.

As if time wound back, I could almost see a soap store, a flower shop, and a few antique and jewelry boutiques across from a café with a vibrant atmosphere.

Now they were but half-burned down, empty shells with blackened façades and shattered glass. Thanks to the devastating war between the demons and the demigods.

I'd lived with my pack in Crack, hidden from the realities of the war and consciously staying away from both dangerous species before Axel found me. I hadn't seen the true devastation of the real world in the age of the Great Merge.

If parts of Manhattan looked like this, how bad must it be for the cities infested by demons?

I swallowed as I strolled down the gutted street. My magic had teleported me here, to a place no one wanted to linger.

Why?

Was this to be my new starting point? Should I rebuild this place for myself?

I stood before a half-broken shop window and stared at my reflection. My clothes were tattered, covered in fresh blood. The pain, though, had dulled. My internal bleeding had stopped, and my bones and tissues had mended.

Even so, new fear brewed in my dark green eyes. The girl staring back at me looked lost.

I wasn't as tough as I'd thought.

I was more vulnerable than I'd like to admit.

I shook my head, banishing fear and uncertainty. First things first, I needed to find a clean outfit. Roaming about like a bloody derelict could attract bad attention.

I jogged around the corner toward an outlet that was relatively intact. It looked like a convenience store. With some luck, I might find something I could use inside.

A chill slithered up my spine, and the small hairs on the back of my neck stood up.

Wind and shadows skittered across the façades of the wrecked stores, surrounding me. A new stench hit my nostrils—acid, sulfur, and brimstone.

My body tensed like a whip, readying to fight, but I had no weapons with me. Dread spread through me as blood pounded in my ears.

The demigods were cruel, merciless beings, but they had at least some humanity in them. And they wanted to preserve human civilization.

Demons, however, were made of pure evil and nothing else.

They had only one intention for humanity—enslaving and destroying it.

I'd thought that fate had finally cut me some slack.

I'd thought that I'd teleported here for a good reason, like this was a place I could claim for myself.

Fate was a sadistic dick.

So here I was with demons closing in.

I halted my pace.

Two horned demons approached me from the front, and a third one that looked more like a troll cut off my escape route from behind.

They were all over seven-feet-tall, wearing scaled armor, their tails thrashing like barbwire. While they had sharp claws and serrated fangs, each one also carried an ax, a spear, or a chainsaw.

Demons didn't fancy swords much because they were favored by their opponents.

Once again, I had no idea how I knew this—or anything else—about demons.

They strutted toward me as if I were a game or a snack.

My gaze swept over them as I attempted to summon my flame and expel the cold terror in my blood. I was wiped out from the fight against both Jack and Paxton, but I needed my power not to fail me now.

I couldn't outrun these three predators.

Shit, I cursed under my breath as I spotted a fourth demon perching atop the roof of a building right above me.

I urgently summoned my power again, waiting for a spark of fire to appear on my sweaty, cold palms.

Please, damn you, just give me a sign you'll aid me.

Magic fizzed in the depths of my well, trying to rise, but all I could access was ember and ash at the bottom.

I'd drained it fighting Paxton, shielding and healing myself, then teleporting here.

I had to improvise until I figured out a plan B.

A green-horned demon clutched a spear in its claws. If I could disarm him and take it, I could even the odds a little.

I needed to entice them to approach first. And I had to do it without showing any fear. Demons preyed and thrived on it.

"Hello, boys, are you lost?" I purred, wheeling around as I endeavored to keep all of them out of my blind spots, though the green-horned demon remained my main target. "I can point you the way home, which is strictly to Hell."

The demons stared at me, surprised expressions flitting through their yellowish and crimson eyes. I bet no one—definitely no human—had called them boys.

"She's funny," a demon with red horns said. "Or she thinks she is."

He flashed me a grin, showing off his sharp, serrated teeth.

"Maybe later, little girl, after we're having a little fun with you," he purred back, which sent bad goosebumps all over my arms.

He wasn't the leader of the band, despite that he carried the scary chainsaw. Demons loved to cart nasty stuff around, anything to inspire fear.

My sweeping gaze landed on a black-horned demon who wielded an ax, clearly the ringleader of this expedition. His black eyes met mine. No mercy, no humanity shone from their depths, just chilling hunger.

"A descendant of the filth of the Earth!" hissed the gray-horned demon from the rooftop.

I'd teleported here in my school uniform, still recognizable despite being bloody and trashed.

I rolled my eyes. "We got a third-class detective here."

The demon jumped from a two-story building and landed to my left. He didn't hold a weapon, but his long, sharp claws glinted like blades.

"Captain, let me kill the little talkative filth so we can get on with our business," he addressed to the black-horned demon.

"Really?" I asked, arching an eyebrow. "Rushing somewhere if not Hell?"

The red-horned demon guffawed, making me wonder if he carried all the humor for the rest of the gang.

"I like this human," he said. "She's got style. I say we play with this pretty little thing first. Let's get her to answer a few questions, like what is she doing in a place no other humans dare set foot in. If she answers well, she gets fucked, then a quick death. But if she stutters...."

"We don't have time to play, Ördög," the gray-horned demon snapped. "We need to find the ultimate weapon and bring it to the great master so we can collect our reward." He stared at me with open disgust. "This filth is a distraction we don't want. One of the demigods has been in the area for two weeks now hunting for the same weapon."

"I'm not afraid of the demigod," the green-horned demon said. "We're four against him."

I inched closer to him for my coveted spear. He was a grade-three demon, like his peers—all except for their captain.

"Naberus is right," the demon captain said, still studying me. "We're lucky to have intercepted the prophecy first, but if we don't get on with our affairs, we'll lose our advantage. The great master wants his prophesied weapon to tilt the scales in our favor. I want a big promotion." He sniffed the air. "This human girl, though, she isn't just an average descendant of the enemies. She smells different than any Olympian I've ever met."

He sniffed the air again.

What the actual fuck?

Why did everyone have a bad habit of sniffing at me?

My bad luck had started with a sniff from a demigod. If Axel hadn't smelled something unique in me back in Crack, he'd never have forced me into the Academy. I never would've been burned, iced over, beaten, and now surrounded by demons in a forsaken street.

The demon captain ranked power-five. He was stronger than all the demons here, as well as the one I'd encountered in the forest.

If I let the demon captain get a better whiff of me, he might drag me to Hell, just as the Demigod of War had dragged me to the Half-Blood Academy.

Without warning, I charged the quiet, green-horned demon, faster than a flash. My fist rammed up to his jaw in a feint.

His yellowish eyes twitched in surprise. A fragile-looking human girl had no business acting so aggressively, from a demon's point of view.

Too bad. I had a flare for shocking people and beings.

While he snarled and lashed out his claws to grab my fist, I yanked on the spear strapped to his left shoulder, spun out of his grasp, then lurched forward and buried the spearhead into his side.

I grinned at myself. I hadn't lost my touch.

He bellowed in pain. I pulled out the spear and leapt back, uncaring that black blood poured out from his gaping wound.

I waved the spear and thrust it toward the captain.

He parried easily, his ax swinging to meet my spear. I stumbled back, hoping the impact didn't cut my palms. His ax followed through, narrowly missing my ear.

My heart pounded in panic as I realized this lot were battle-trained demons.

Two other demons closed in, one from my left and the other from my back. The wounded green-horned demon served as their backup, shouting for my blood.

The situation didn't look great for me.

Just as the gang was about to thrust their weapons at me, all at the same time, and I was about to duck attacks from all directions to my best ability, the captain shouted. "Halt!"

The minions stopped in their tracks, but kept their weapons up around me, ready to resume stabbing holes in my person as soon as their boss gave the go ahead.

The captain sniffed the air yet again, and his black horns twisted and hissed like snakes.

He creeped me out.

His goons followed suit and inhaled the air, too. Their pitiless eyes now rolled with astonishment and confusion.

"If she's the one, our banishment will come to an end when we offer her to the great master," the leader said, his black eyes swirling with foul darkness.

He spoke in a demonic tongue to his lackeys, yet I understood all of it, as if the evil language was etched in my bones and flowed in my blood.

A chilling panic filled my mind.

No one could understand the demonic language, not even the demigods, unless they were a demon. But I couldn't be a demon, could I?

No demon could step through the wards of the Academy, yet I'd dwelled in the center of the school grounds with the Olympian girls. The Ritual of the Blood Runes would burn a demon to ashes, but—

My breathed shortened.

The runes had burned me mercilessly, but I hadn't turned into a pile of ash. Instead, I'd survived and gained power greater than any descendant's.

Yet my fire didn't seem to be from any of the twelve Olympian gods' houses.

And now this sorry-ass, demon rogue band was taking an uncanny interest in me.

"Can she really be…the Lost Princess?" the red-horned demon asked with reverence.

No! Terror struck me. I couldn't be a demon spawn, even though I had been lost on the street when Vi found me.

"There is this rumor in the Underworld that no one even dares to whisper…" murmured the gray-horned demon as he looked at me in a different light.

The demon captain snapped, sweeping them with a harsh look. "Say no more. I won't lose my head because of you fools' loose tongues."

"We're finally having good luck, right?" asked the red-horned demon hopefully. "I mean, she just fell into our laps like this? I'm sick and tired of being called a loser."

"You three keep looking for the weapon," the demon captain said sternly, his eyes roaming my every inch while he sniffed me again. "I'll take the girl and get her ready."

He'd drag me to the core of Hell.

I wheeled and swung my spear up toward his neck.

I realized that demons could take a lot of damage. It'd be a bad strategy to wound them here and there with small holes, an effort that would soon wear me down. The best strategy was to strike as hard as I could, weaken them, and then make my escape.

And now I had one advantage—the demons wanted to capture me instead of kill me.

The captain brought up his ax to parry, but I shifted my angle.

My spear sank into his throat.

He ducked, but not quickly enough—probably because he was daydreaming about me being his ticket to a better life.

My spear left a thin trail of oozing black blood around his neck.

He bellowed in rage, darkness twirling eerily inside his eyes.

"I'll kill you if you prove more trouble than you're worth, little girl," he hissed.

"And we'll bury the secret of killing the possible Lost One," the green-horned demon echoed, totally onboard. I figured he hated me for stabbing him.

Three demons closed ranks, no longer worried that they might severely injury me.

The chainsaw cut into my back below my shoulder blade.

Screaming, I tore myself away from the jagged metal, sidestepped, booted the captain, and wheeled toward the red-horned demon.

The gruesome chainsaw dripped with my blood.

With a furious roar and a burst of strength, I tossed my spear toward the red-horned demon's throat. I aimed true, and it pierced the demon's neck.

He widened his eyes in disbelief before he dropped in a heap, his chainsaw flying from his hands. His red horns scratched the ground with a coarse scrape.

Before I could snatch his chainsaw or yank out the spear from his throat, the other demons charged.

Things didn't look too hot for me.

Harsh, urgent flapping sounds beat into the wind. A vast shadow flitted over us, blotting out the sky.

Goddamnit! More demons were coming.

I dared not look up as I trained all my attention on the gang that was now determined to cut me to pieces.

I would jump on the wounded, green-horned demon next.

"A demigod!" shrieked the gray-eyed demon.

Had Axel or Zak tracked me down?

A sliver of hope rose in me. It would suck to return to the Academy, but it was better than going to Hell.

"We grab her and shift to our domain," the demon captain barked. "One, two...."

They slammed into me.

I roared in dread, shoving them off.

As a claw sank into my skin, latching onto my arm, a wave of black wind and light tore the demons from me.

A demon's razor-sharp claw slid through my hair and then dropped to the ground, cleaved from its hand by a long black blade.

A pair of mighty obsidian wings flung demons away from me.

A formidable, gorgeous warrior with the face of an angel descended from the sky above and planted himself in front of me, his sapphire eyes burning with dark, heavenly fire.

CHAPTER 14
Demigod of Death

She stood there, my lamb, the girl from my dreams.

Her lush, lavender hair flew wildly in the electric wind, her full pink lips pulled back in a snarl, and her green eyes that made the rest of the world seem pale burned with unquenchable fire.

Her touch had created a firestorm in my blood.

She was the first woman who had touched me and lived, even in my dreams.

My heart, which had never beaten for anyone, pounded in my chest. For her, my blood heated in my ancient, icy veins, just as it had in my dreams.

I saw only her, nothing and no one else, until her roar brought me out of my trance.

I now noticed the rest of the scene.

Four demons surrounded her in the demolished street, closing in to maim and capture her.

Instead of cowering, my brave lamb waved a spear, like a warrior made of fire. She poured her rage out as she thrust the spearhead toward her foes.

Acid fire twisted my innards as I noted her own blood covering her academy uniform.

She'd been beaten and tortured.

Wrath filled my being.

Her enemies would pay. I'd tear them apart for what they did to my lamb.

My black wings summoned the wind.

She was mine to protect and then to claim, possess, and keep forever.

I'd been haunting Manhattan, the beast's belly, in search of the coveted weapon a prophecy said would appear at these coordinates.

A weapon called the living flame would tilt the scales of the war between Hell and Heaven. I wouldn't allow such a weapon to fall into Lucifer's hands.

So far I hadn't found the weapons—not even a trace of it. But now I'd found the treasure of my heart.

I'd found my mate.

With black wind on my ebony wings and a fiery black longsword in my grip, I tore into the horde of the demons to shield my lamb.

I was the Demigod of Death, and I would never allow death to touch her.

CHAPTER 15

My dream lover had flown out of my dream and materialized in front of me.

I gazed up at him, my eyes wild with shock and raw need.

The wind he'd brought down to Earth tousled his rich brown hair, framing his stunningly beautiful and masculine face. His strong figure could've been carved right out of pure, hard ice, and his spirit shone like a deadly flame tracing dangerously beneath the glacier.

His firm, curvy lips were just like I'd remembered—kissable.

His sapphire eyes, brimming with concern, rage, joy, and disbelief, gazed down at me. As his gaze paused on the blood all over my academy uniform, wrath iced over his eyes.

"You're real," I stuttered.

The savage world and the demons all faded away. It was just him and me.

My ravenous gaze roved over his taut torso wrapped in silver and black armor. When I'd met him in the dream, he'd been bare-chested.

Then he'd been naked beneath me.

I'd seen his massive, gorgeous shaft, the first cock I'd ever touched.

For a second, my mind was filled with the image of his steel rod prodding at my entrance before thrusting into my heated core.

I'd glided down his hard length, like nothing else mattered.

I'd ridden him like the wildest thing on Earth, and he'd bucked his powerful hips up and thrust into me with abandon.

His every hard inch had stretched my inner muscles deliciously while my sex gloved his cock perfectly and tightly.

His scent of pure male, cinder, and night had infused my bloodstream.

He'd fucked me. He'd unmade me before I'd been yanked out of the dream.

I'd never thought he could be real, though I'd wished with every piece of my soul that he somehow existed.

In my moments of blind rage, panic, and despair in the Hall

of Olympia, I'd had no one to turn to. I'd had nowhere to go. I guess when I'd reached out to him, hoping to escape the real world, I'd magically teleported directly to him.

Not exactly directly.

I blinked back to the battlefield on the cracked street, watching my tender dream lover transform into a ferocious, formidable warrior.

"I'm real," he said, his rich, deep voice caressing me. The heat in his eyes burned the short fuse between us. "So are you, lamb. Finding you satisfies me more than anything."

As soon as he called me lamb, I knew he was absolutely real, and he was here for me, to defend me. Tears flooded my eyes, stinging my eyelids.

He smiled at me, brightening my existence. His intense gaze dipped to my lips, as if he wanted to sweep me into his arms and kiss me more than anything. The raw need and tenderness in his galaxy-sapphire eyes, though, vanished in the next heartbeat, replaced by icy fury.

"Let me get rid of these foul beings before we resume our lovely affair," he said. His deep, musical voice chilled, his tone chipped with the hardest ice. "They'll regret that they ever laid a claw on you."

Like a black storm, he tore through my attackers. His longsword gleamed with dark flame as it cleaved a demon's gray horn.

My knight wanted to punish my foes first. He thought these demons had made me bleed, that they were the cause of the blood that soaked my uniform.

I restrained myself from cheering at his magnificent fighting style. Even the best warrior might lose their footing when distracted.

The gray-horned demon screamed in pain before my knight decapitated him with one clean, swift sweep of his sword. And then without turning, my dream lover drove his blade backward, impaling the green-horned demon as the demon jumped on him, fangs bared and claws out.

I'd never seen anyone fight so superbly. I considered myself a good fighter, if given a weapon, but I was barely in his league.

Now only the demon captain remained.

"Rest, lamb," my knight said softly. "I'll join you in no time."

He didn't need my help, and I was fatigued and in pain from the new wound below my shoulder where the demon's nasty chainsaw had cut me.

I held my chin high, signaling that I, Marigold, allowed my knight to battle on my behalf. I jogged toward the red-horned demon's corpse and yanked the spear from his throat. Then I slouched onto a ruptured boulder, my ankle crossed over my knee, and watched my defender ram his sword into the demon captain's ax.

The sharp rake of metal on metal echoed along the street as fire sparked off their steel.

The duelers moved in a blur, hacking, chopping, and battering at each other with unforgiving force.

I couldn't take my eyes off the fight, and my knight seemed to relish the attention. Each flourish of his weapon was as elegant as it was deadly, like a fight choreographed to not just win, but impress me—his rapt audience—and to offer me every satisfaction.

He lunged at the demon like the fastest wind, booting the captain in the gut and sending him to crash against the façade of a store that used to sell cheap perfumes. The impact brought down the rest of the wall and half of the ceiling. Concrete, dirt, and wooden beams rained down on the demon captain.

I loved it! It was like watching an action movie unfolding right in front of me.

My knight wanted to punish this demon captain for me prior to killing him.

Before the captain could get to his feet, my knight grabbed him and flung him across the street. The demon's horns pierced a brick column, and his fall dented the ground.

"Oops, that hurt," I shouted.

The demon tossed his ax at my knight before I finished my cheer.

A warning tore from my throat, but my man snatched the hilt of the spinning ax out of the air easily. Menace and fury rolling off him, he stalked toward the demon with predatory purpose, ready to cut down his opponent and wrap up this episode.

Suddenly, the demon captain grinned at me. His intentions clicked, and horror grabbed me.

The demon was going to make an exit.

He believed I was some kind of lost legend—there was no way he'd quit this hunt. If he escaped, he'd come back for me.

Worse, if he reported me to more powerful demons, the horde would join him until they had their claws in me. Though I didn't think I was their lost princess—I wasn't any fucking princess—it wouldn't stop those greedy demon bastards from attempting to drag me to Hell.

"Don't let him get away!" I shrieked and charged toward the demon captain with the spear thrust in front of me.

My knight moved in a blur at the same time.

Our weapons slammed toward the demon, but he shifted to smoke and vanished.

I stared at the empty space where the demon captain had been as cold dread and dismay filled me.

"Worry no more, lamb," my knight commanded. "With me guarding you, no one will ever harm a single hair on your head."

He swept his sapphire eyes to the sky, the roofs, and the rest of our surroundings and, finding no more threats, gazed down at me with all the protectiveness and possessiveness in the world.

My chest warmed. My heart fluttered.

I stepped toward him eagerly. I needed to touch him and feel for myself that he was one hundred percent real and he was here.

His sapphire eyes brightened. At first he opened his arms, ready to pull me into his embrace, but then he stiffened. Staggering away from me, he tucked his obsidian wings in tightly.

"No, lamb," he whispered, his expression pained. "Don't touch me."

I halted, feeling like he'd doused me in icy water. I'd thought he wanted me.

He saw the hurt in my eyes, and agony distorted his gorgeous face.

"You were all over me in the dream," I accused, lashing out as the hurt of rejection sank even deeper into my bones. "Guess you're just a phony. I was wrong about you. I shouldn't have sought you out."

"You sought me out?"

"I came here for you, didn't I?" I said bitterly.

He blinked in confusion. "How did you know I was here?"

"I didn't know you were here," I said. "But I thought of you before I teleported."

A swirl of dark stars glimmered in his eyes. "You don't know who I am, do you?"

Judging by the scorching desire etched into every line in his face, he wanted me. But then why did he want to confuse me?

I braced a hand on my hip. "I met you only once before and that was in a dream. You never told me who you are, though I asked, and then I was yanked right out of the dream."

"I'm Héctor," he said in sorrow and defeat. "I'm the death demigod. No one can touch me and live because my skin is lethal to everyone."

I widened my eyes in utter shock.

My dream lover was the Demigod of Death, my supposed enemy?

He held my gaze, scrutinizing my every tiny reaction and emotion to his words, and I had the impression that he was waiting for me to run from him.

"I'm sorry, lamb, you can't touch me." He sighed in resignation. "We can only be with each other in a dream. If it's good for you, that's good enough for me. I'll protect you day and night. You'll be the only woman for me in dreams and in life."

I studied the tensed line on his gorgeous face as he held his breath, expecting me to deny him.

I had defied every rule in the book.

So I was going to defy this one last, inconvenient rule.

If I could touch him in the dream, I could touch him anywhere.

The Ritual of the Blood Runes hadn't burned me to ash, and the touch of the death demigod wouldn't reduce me to a cracked clay statue either.

I wouldn't accept that I could only have him in my dreams, not after I'd met him in the flesh. And no one could choose what dreams they would get on any given night. I needed more than those few lucky moments with him.

"I crave your touch more than anything," he said, angst brimming in his eyes. "But—"

I shoved my palm against his jaw before he could stop me.

"No, lamb! What have you done?" he cried out in horror, his eyes wide with devastation.

But I didn't drop dead.

Only a river of pleasure buzzed over my skin. His fresh stubble pricking against the heel of my palm felt delicious.

"Uh, sorry," I said, grinning at him. "I hit you a bit too hard, but you didn't give me much of choice."

He stared at me, dumbfounded.

Reluctantly, I withdrew my hand from his face, but he caught my wrist and brought my palm to his lips.

"You can touch me, lamb," he said incredulously. My dream guy looked like the Demigod of Joy instead of the Demigod of Death. "You can really touch me."

I laughed in victory. "I told you, silly."

I hadn't told him. I'd just acted.

A sexy, amused smile ghosted his lips. "No one has ever called the death demigod silly. No one dared."

"I dared," I said. "I—"

He swept me into his arms with such passionate force that I widened my eyes in giddiness.

"You're mine, my brave lamb," he announced.

He dipped his head and slanted his mouth over mine.

Heat radiated like a hot sun from him to me, and liquid flame erupted between my thighs.

With death's kiss, life blossomed in me.

Half-Blood Academy 2: Magic Secret
Coming in July 2019

SNEAK PEEK:
A COURT OF BLOOD AND VOID

A lineup of vampires waited before the magnificent entrance of the mansion. A dark-haired beauty who carried herself like a vampire queen stood out the most. She wore an elegant silver gown worth more than a working-class family's annual income.

I kind of hated rich people.

The vampires bowed at Lorcan as we stepped out of the car. "High Lord."

The striking beauty stepped toward Lorcan, her gray gaze glued to his face, greedily taking in his every line.

A sudden jealousy stabbed me. I wanted to slap her.

"Welcome home, my lord," the beauty said, her gaze flicking to me for a nanosecond before returning to Lorcan. Her world had only him.

"Who are you?" I stepped forward, refusing to let anyone dismiss me.

The beauty glared at me with icy hostility. Vampires were the most unfriendly creatures anyway.

"This is Mistress Selena, dulcis," Lorcan said.

Selena's eyes widened at Lorcan's endearment.

"Mistress?" I narrowed my eyes at Lorcan, anger and humiliation sizzling in me. "Like she's your concubine? Why wasn't I informed?"

And how dare he take my blood and claim me when he already had a woman at home!

"Selena administers my realm when I'm away," Lorcan said. "I trust her to care for my land. She's loyal and excels in all things, but she doesn't share my bed."

"Then who shares your bed?" I demanded, black fire twirling in my eyes.

"*You, dulcis*, only you," he said, amusement sparkling in his gray eyes at my tone.

"Oh," I said, feeling my face flaming. I stepped back. One had to know when to fight and when to withdraw.

"Don't retreat yet," Lorcan said, pulling me to him, his hand circling my waist. "I haven't introduced you. These are my most trusted inner circle. You'll get to know them." He then turned to Selena and his inner circle vampires. "High Lady Cass Saélihn is my chosen mate. You'll treat her as such."

All the vampires' eyes widened before they covered up their astonishment in the nick of time. Have I mentioned that I have super eyesight and reflexes? I didn't miss anything, nor did I miss the pure hatred in Selena's eyes.

Being her High Lord's mate had made me her number one enemy. As long as she didn't act on it, I'd let it slide.

"Cass is not only my mate, but the mate to all of my bonded brothers," Lorcan added, sweeping a hand toward Alaric, Pyrder, and Reysalor, who maintained steely cold expressions.

They knew how to deal with bloodsuckers.

I should have used the same look in front of the vampires rather than my customary sneer, but it was too late to wipe my sneer off now, so I turned it to a smirk.

The vampires remained still and didn't even blink naturally.

"My mate and my brothers need to settle in," Lorcan said sternly. "We'll hold a meeting in an hour."

"Yes, High Lord." The vampires bowed again.

A vampire butler led us into the mansion, which was the finest in every way. I looked left and right and up at the ceilings, awed, before I grinned at Lorcan.

"I hope my home is up to your standards," Lorcan said, his arm never leaving my waist.

"It's above average," I said.

"It's your home now," he said.

"In that case, I hope the cuisine is up to par too, at least better than the mediocre food in ShadesStar court."

Lorcan shook his head, a smile ghosting his sensual lips. "Dulcis is hard to impress."

Then I was in Alaric's arms.

All the males had long legs, and Alaric was sparing me from sprinting. I enjoyed pressing my breasts against his cut chest anyway, so I let him carry me all the way until we entered a vast suite that had connected five rooms and one large common room.

The sleeping quarters were perfect for us.

The guards stayed outside the door, so only the five of us were in the common room.

"I built this suite to honor the pact a millennium ago," Lorcan said, his heated eyes on me before he swept a glance at Reys, Alaric, and Pyrder. "Only now, finally, it's put to its full use."

"I want the largest room that has a full-window view," I said before anyone else could stake a claim.

The males chuckled.

"You don't need your own room, Cass baby," Pyrder said. "All the rooms are yours. You'll just pick a different bed to sleep on every night."

My face flamed as blood heated in me.

"Since we're all your mates," Alaric drawled, "you'll learn to balance us and treat us equally if you don't want fights to break out among us."

I narrowed my eyes at him. If it got too hard, I'd just quit!

"No, no," Alaric said, as if he read my thought. "You'll never quit on us, sweetheart."

Before I could stand up for myself and fight back against his dominance, he grabbed me and crushed me to his hard chest. Wasting no time, he dipped his head and slanted his mouth against mine.

His scent of pine, leather, and oil painting wrapped around me, both gentle and harsh. His kiss was raw, hard, and tender. Only the demigod could administer such contradictory kisses.

My mates were so different from one another. Even the twin fae didn't share many traits, though they had the same features and turquoise eyes. And yet Pyrder's eyes were a shade darker, and he had a tattoo of a golden panther on his forearm and half of his chest. One day, hopefully soon, I'd get a chance to explore him as well and get a good look at the entire panther.

Alaric's kiss deepened. His tongue thrust into my mouth, tasting me, and I twirled mine around him, tasting him back. He had lightning in him, compatible with my fire, yet the two elements tended to compete, which caused many sparks between the demigod and me.

I melted into him, forgetting why I'd been fighting him a minute ago.

"It's not entertainment time." Reysalor's deep voice rang beside us. "Let's settle in first. We have serious business."

If he had his tongue down my throat, he wouldn't have mentioned this "serious business." Alaric obviously thought the same. He sucked my tongue playfully and erotically before releasing me, though I didn't want release since fire was coursing in my bloodstream.

Displeased with the cold, empty air on my lips, I turned to Reys with a glare.

Reys only pulled me to him and kissed my lips hot and hard before letting me go. I instantly forgot my anger and gazed up at him longingly. The scene of me riding him and him giving me oral pleasure reeled back. I hadn't been as close to Reys as I'd wanted since all my mates had shown up, and Reys was my first best friend.

"You'll have all of us soon, Cass baby," Reys said with a wink. "We're all yours."

I wondered if I would have them one-on-one or all at the same time, as in that dream I had, but I had no time to ponder that since we had to rush to the vampires' meeting.

To be honest, I'd rather have taken a nap, or cuddled with one of my males, which would certainly lead to further exploration and fireworks, than attend a meeting. But my new role seemed to require me to take part in all the activities of my alpha males if I didn't want to be left behind.

More Books by Meg Xuemei X

THE FIRST WITCH SERIES

OF SHADOWS AND FIRE SERIRS

THE WAR OF GODS SERIES

HALF-BLOOD ACADEMY SERIES

THE CURSED DRAGON QUEEN & HER MATES

EMPRESS OF MYSTH SERIES

TRUE MATE SERIES

THE WICKEDEST WITCH SERIES

DARK CHEMISTRY SERIES

The Girl Next Door: A Small Town Romance

About the Author

Meg Xuemei X is a USA Today bestselling author of steamy fantasy and paranormal romance. She finds it dreamingly delightful to be around drop-dead gorgeous alpha males who are forever tormented by her feisty heroines, formidable alien fallen angels, wild shifters, unseelie fae, dark vampires, menacing demigods, and cunning witches.

She is always happy to hear from readers and welcome new friends on Facebook.
Email: megxuemei@gmail.com

Made in United States
Troutdale, OR
10/27/2023